# OUTLAWS AWAKENED

## A REAPERS WINGS NOVEL

### RAVEN GULLEY

Editing-CookieLynn Publishing Services

Book Cover Design- Miblart

ONE

## CASH

FOR FIVE YEARS I've been the President of the Reapers Wings Motorcycle Club and it's been the best five years of my life. I love what I do and what the club stands for. My brothers, aka the club members, are the best thing that has ever happened to me. Being their leader gives me purpose for belonging on this earth. It makes me believe that's the reason I was born.

Every single one of us are criminals and have a record, even though they are only minor offenses. It would be hard to be in this club and your record be squeaky clean. We are criminals but just because we have done and do bad things doesn't make us bad people.

Most of us have been arrested for stupid shit like driving under the influence and aggravated assault. Every single person we have assaulted deserved it. It's just too bad the police and judge didn't think otherwise.

Things have been quiet here in Heartwood Springs the past ten years and I hope things stay that way. Up until ten years ago, the Southern Demons – a rival club and the real criminals – had also occupied this town.

The Southern Demons are nothing but pieces of shit—a white supremacy group who sell drugs, rob banks, serve as hitmen, and other criminal activity. I wish I could kill every single one of them. Unfortunately, there are far too many of them. They have charters all throughout the confederate states. The only thing they care about is making money and will go to great lengths to get that cash.

Our job at Reapers Wings is to keep the people in Heartwood Springs safe by keeping criminal activity out of our town, even though it's not always possible.

Ever since the Southern Demons left, things have been much better. We have had more peace than we ever had before. Crime has been at an all-time low and things have been amazing. People have come to respect us now more than ever. They know we have their interest in mind and realize just how good we truly are.

I have lived my entire life here in Heartwood Springs, and it's the place that I plan to live until I'm buried in my grave. I love it here because it's my home. There will never be another place like it on this earth. So I'll be damned if anyone comes here and tries to destroy my town again. They will have to get through me and my brothers first and we aren't people to fuck around with.

I hold the door open for Darcy and the two of us step outside.

"Are you sure that you don't need me to work tonight?" Darcy, my old lady for the past six months, gets ready to hop in her red sports car.

I love her more than anything in this world. She's the woman who I want to have my children. The woman I plan on proposing to, when it's the right time. It just so happens she also works for me at Reapers Wings Bar and Grill.

"I'm sure. Now you better get going before I change my

mind."

Darcy plants a kiss on my lips, before reaching for the door handle. "I'll call you later."

"If you don't then I'm going to come looking."

Tonight is the first night that Darcy has wanted a night off since she started working for me. She is the one person I can count on to handle things at the bar. I have never had anyone as fast as her whip up mixed drinks or hand out beers. On some of the nights I had worked with her, she was doing circles around me. After that night, I let her have it all to herself, and told her if she needed me to call. Not once had I heard from her that night so she had handled herself well.

Darcy and I grew up together, since our fathers were both in the mc. We also went to school together and remained great friends over the years. We remained such great friends that when she moved to Texas, I had even visited her a couple of times. Last year she decided she wanted to move back and was looking for a place to say. So I had let her stay with me until she got a few things figured out.

Fast forward six months later, she landed herself in jail for assaulting a woman. I was there when it happened and it was the funniest shit I've ever seen. Imagine a petite blonde woman starting a fight with a woman two times bigger than her. The fight had happened because the woman had been texting and driving. She had the misfortune of hitting Darcy's car in the process. I had bailed Darcy out of jail and the two of us have been a thing ever since.

She taps her finger on my nose. "Are you going to be at the clubhouse later or at home?"

"Right here." I press my lips against hers one last time. She had spent extra time on her makeup and had even curled her hair. She looks so damn fine that I squeeze her ass. The world needs to know she is mine. "Now go and enjoy yourself."

She gives me the stink eye. "You better stay out of trouble."

"I can't make any promises to that."

She stifles a grin. "On that note, I am leaving."

I slap her ass before she gets in her car. "Bye, sweetheart."

Martin gets off his motorcycle and whistles. "I guess you forgot to mention how we are all going to get fucked up tonight."

I didn't forget to mention anything. She knows Pete was getting out of jail today, which meant we were all partying until the sun came up. There was nothing quite like booze and pussy. They were two things in this world that would never get old.

I'm not going to partake in any sexual activities with a woman unless it's Darcy. I'm not a cheater and never will be. You can't love someone and cheat on them.

"The two of us have trust in our relationship. I don't need to mention anything."

Martin removes his helmet and gets off his motorcycle. "I still don't see how you didn't tap that in high school. She's sexier than hell."

I am just going to ignore his comment. It doesn't upset me or make me angry; it's just he could have a woman too if he really wanted a woman. But his head stays in his ass and he doesn't seem interested in finding a good woman. Instead, he just likes having hookups and one-night stands with women who mean nothing to him. He is the definition of what I used to be until Darcy came along.

"I wasn't ready for that in high school. We would have

never lasted."

Martin takes out a pack of cigarettes from his leather cut and lights one. "I take it that you're about to meet Nancy at the cemetery."

It has been ten years since my father was murdered by the Southern Demons. The day had started out like any other day here in Heartwood Springs. Little did I know when the day was over, I would never see him alive again.

My father and his brothers tried to stop the Southern Demons from robbing the Heartwood Springs Credit Union. He was shot and killed instantly.

The guys who were there at the Heartwood Springs Credit Union went to prison and will never get out in this lifetime. I wish we could have gotten revenge for my father's murder. It would have made the pain of losing him more bearable, but they are in prison where they belong.

"I am and I'm running late, so I better get going." I put on my helmet and then get on my motorcycle. "I'll see you later."

Nancy, my mother, is a damn good woman. She is a Christian and never misses a day of church unless she's on vacation which isn't often. All other Sundays she is right there praising God. Things haven't always been that way though. My father's murder had brought her closer to God. It was the only way she had known how to deal with his death.

Martin knows I'm on a time crunch because it's the same time Nancy and I meet every year. "See you later man. Give Nancy a hug for me."

I crank up my motorcycle and get ready to pull out of the driveway. "That's something I will do."

The town is busting with traffic and I wish that I would have left the clubhouse sooner. I'm going to be a couple of minutes late, but I know Nancy won't care. She'll just be grateful I showed up. She didn't like going to the Reapers Wings Cemetery all alone.

I can't say that I like going to visit my father since he's dead. He will never breathe or walk this earth again. I will never be able to have a conversation with him. I don't see what the point is, visiting a dead man. The sole reason I come is because of Nancy. She needs me here.

For as long as I can remember, my father had always been a member of the Reapers Wings Motorcycle Club. Back then, when I was a little boy, I remember spending most of my time at the clubhouse while Nancy and Ray worked.The Reapers Wings Cemetery hasn't always been here in Heartwood Springs. Back in 1979, when one of the very first members of the club had died, the cemetery was born. My grandfather, Lee Daniels, one of the very first members of the club, had wanted a special place for all of the Reapers Wings to be buried. So he had formed the graveyard with his ten acres of land.

Martin and Bryce maintain the cemetery. They spend multiple hours here every week making sure that it looks nice. Looking around at the fresh cut grass and the low-cut brush makes me pleased. The two of them did a hell of a good job making it look great.

I turn off my motorcycle and see Nancy is already at Ray's grave. Tears stream down her face, and my heart aches for her. Dad had been the love of her life. The two of them were together ever since high school.

"I'm glad that you're here, Cash."

I wrap my arms around her in a hug, hoping to give her comfort. "I couldn't let you be alone on a day like today."

She pushes the tears away with her hand. "I wish that he was still here with us, but we will see him again."

I'm not so sure about that. I never did remember Dad getting baptized or going to church. But I'm not going to burst Nancy's bubble. I'll let her think what she wants.

"I sure do hope so, because I miss him." I would always miss him, but it wasn't something I could dwell on. Too much anger consumed me, since he should still be alive today. "I would do anything to talk to or see him again."

"Can I ask you something, Cash?" Nancy places the flowers that are in her hand on Ray's grave. "It's something I've been meaning to talk to you about for a while, but never got a chance to."

"Of course. You can ask me anything."

"I want you to go to church with me."

That answer is definitely a no. I do not like going to church and never will.

"I don't know about that, Nancy." I want to talk about anything else except for this. It was something she brought up every time we were together. "I'm not the definition of a church goer."

She doesn't try to hide the disappointment on her face. "You're not going to live forever, Cash. None of us are."

She's telling me something I already know. The last thing I want to think about is death and dying. I'm only thirty-five.

"Nancy, you do enough praying for the two of us."

It's true. She prays more than anybody I know.

"Promise me you will at least read your Bible."

On my birthday last year, she had gotten me a Bible. I still hadn't picked it up and read a word of it. But I'm not much of a reader.

I nod. "I promise I'll try to."

Just because I say it doesn't mean I will. I just want to get her off my back.

She knows I don't want to have this conversation. It's the reason she changes the subject. "I heard through the grapevine Pete got out of jail."

The grapevine is Pete's grandma, Edith. It is no surprise she would mention it, considering the two of them go to church together.

"He did. I'm going to the clubhouse after we get done here." I don't like not being there when Pete makes his grand appearance. But I know he would understand my reasoning behind it. "I'll probably stay there for a few days."

It's no secret that we are going to be partying it up. She doesn't approve of it but isn't about to mention it.

"Are you and Darcy still together?" The question doesn't surprise me. It's been a couple of weeks since we've sat down to have a conversation.

Now is the perfect time to show her the engagement ring. "Darcy and I have never been better." I get the engagement ring out of my jean pocket. "I'm ready to ask her to marry me."

Her head snaps to me, blonde hair fluttering around her face, at the mention of us getting married. I'm late getting started in that department. Not once in my life have I ever been serious enough to settle down with a woman. "I'm happy that you've found somebody. Now, hopefully soon, I can start hounding you for grandkids."

I laugh. Last month Darcy got off the pill because we have been talking about starting a family. "The thing is, Nancy, I'm not sure when I'm going to propose to her."

"I'm sure that it will be sometime soon." She takes the ring out of my hand to get a closer look at it. Her eyes widen at how big the diamond is. It's not like I would get

Darcy a cheap ring. She is my queen and deserves something nice. "I don't even want to know how much that ring cost."

"Good, because I don't want you to have a heart attack."

Her having a heart attack was bound to happen, considering the ring was five thousand dollars.

"Don't you go proposing to her without me there. We need to take lots of pictures. It's a day that needs to be documented."

Nancy has always been big on taking pictures.

"I'll let you know what I have planned."

It is one promise I can keep my word on.

She wraps her arms around me and gives me a bear hug. It's something she always does before we part ways. "Your father would be so proud of you, Cash. I know we might not agree on some things, but I am proud of you too. I don't care what anyone says about you, you are a good man. No matter what happens with this club, or anything else, don't ever let that change."

I don't think that she would be so quick to call me good if she knew all the things I have done. I wouldn't like to consider myself a monster, but I have killed people before. I can't say that I enjoyed it, but I don't regret it either.

Tears press at the back of my eyes, but I force them back, refusing to let them fall. An immovable lump forms in my throat and I cough, trying to rein in my emotions. "Nancy, you didn't have to go and say all of that now."

"I just told you the truth, Cash." She lets go of me. "Because it's something you needed to hear."

"I'm grateful that you are my mother and the woman who raised me."

I couldn't even think about having another woman as a mother. I love Nancy more than anything in this world. She has showed me what love truly means. She is the reason I respect women, even if we don't see eye to eye on things.

A sad expression crosses her face. "I'm so ready for your brother Rich to be home."

I knew him being in jail was causing her heartache.

"We've only got a month left until he's out." I couldn't wait for him to be back. Not only was he my brother, he is also my best friend. Things haven't been the same since he has been behind bars. "It doesn't seem like those four weeks can get here fast enough."

"The house feels so empty with the two of you gone." I feel bad for Nancy being all alone. It does make me worry about her. "I might start dropping in and staying with you. I don't like being all alone. Everything being so quiet drives me crazy."

I bought a house two years ago, and Rich lives at the clubhouse when he's not locked up.

"You're always welcome in my house and at the clubhouse anytime." But she already knows that. "Ray wouldn't want you to be all alone, Nancy. You should think about dating again."

At only fifty-three, Nancy is much too young to spend the rest of her life alone. Rich and I both are all for her having a boyfriend as long as he treats her right and isn't an enemy of the club.

She shakes her head like she does every time I bring it up. "The love of my life was your father. You and Rich are the only two men in my life that I need."

"Ray would want you to be happy." I don't say it to upset her. I just say it because it's the truth. "That's all Rich and I want you to be too."

"I am happy, Cash. I just wish you boys wouldn't have grown up."

Darcy and I definitely need to give her some grandkids.

I press my fingers to my lips and put it across Ray's headstone. If only he could have lived a little while longer. "I guess I am going to head out, Nancy."

She gives me one final hug. "Call me this week and I'll come running."

I'm not going to call her. Instead, I am going to show up at her house unannounced. "I will. Don't worry."

"I think that it's time for me and your father to be alone."

Which meant that it was time for me to leave.

I squeeze her shoulder. "Don't stay out here too long."

She nods. "I'll see you later, Cash."

---

PETE

For a man who has been locked up for the past five months, you would think I would be happy to be out of jail. I sure am happy to have my freedom and be back with my brothers. What I am not happy about is that my girlfriend Natalie and I aren't together anymore.

"Do you want to talk about her brother?" Slash is the one who picks me up from Heartwood Springs Regional Jail. Out of all the boys, he's the one I'm closest with. "I know that she has to be on your mind."

"I just don't get how she could end things with me after ten years of being together." Sure, I had gone to jail for assault, but she knew she was taking a walk with the devil when the two of us got together. "It's almost as if our relationship didn't mean shit to her."

"Back then, the two of you were only eighteen. She probably just doesn't want to be a part of club life anymore."

I know her well enough to know that she loved being a club member's old lady. It was the reason the two of us had gotten together ten years ago in the first place. There's something more to the story. I just have to find out what.

"I guess it's time for me to move on." I hate saying it or even thinking about it. I thought that the two of us were going to get married and grow old together. But she had proven me wrong. "I won't be able to move on without talking to her first."

"You're not going to change her mind, Pete." Slash normally knows what he's talking about. But he doesn't know what he's talking about when it comes to this. "I would suggest you just her let go. There are so many other women you can be with."

"Is there something you need to tell me?" Now he really has me going. I'm not about to let this go.

"The first time I went to prison my ex-wife got together with another man." Slash clears his throat. "I'm thinking that may be the case with yours."

His words hit me like I've been knocked out by a ton of bricks. Our relationship had to mean more than that to her. Because it did to me. She is the love of my life, or I thought she was.

Him using his ex-wife Nicole was a horrible example. Despite her cheating on him, the two of them got married again several years later after being divorced for four years. "But you still ended up remarrying Nicole after everything she'd done to you."

"I wish I wouldn't have. It would have saved me the heartache." He looks at me a brief second before turning his attention back to the road. "Don't be foolish and make the same mistakes I did just because you love her."

The heartache he's talking about is the death of their

son, Aaron, who died four years ago. He had drowned at the pool in town. Nicole had left him for just a couple of minutes to go get them food from the concession stand. When she came back, none of the lifeguards had been watching him and he was already under water. He was just a kid of six, and it had been a sad time for everyone.

"I'm so sorry about your son, Slash. I know his birthday is coming up."

He was born on August tenth. I remember the day just like it was yesterday. It was nothing but sunshine and clear skies. I sure did miss the little fellow, and I knew Slash did too.

"Let's not forget we are talking about you here, not me. I don't want to be filled with grief, pain, or anger today, Pete."

"I don't want to be angry today either."

The only thing that I want to be today is happy.

He seems pretty sure of himself. "Did she come visit you while you were in jail?"

I didn't need to tell him the answer to that because he already knows. "No. I just called her once, hoping to get back together with her. But she didn't even answer her phone."

"I'm telling you, and I know you don't want to hear it, but she's found someone else."

"Have you seen her around town with another man?" I have a feeling his answer is going to be no.

"I didn't need to see her around town to know she's with someone else." So that was his way of saying I was in denial. "You haven't heard a word from her and she didn't volunteer to pick you up today. If I had a guess, she has all your bags packed, ready for you to come and get them."

I could clearly see the reason why we were heading to my house now. The house that I would no longer be staying at until Natalie and I could work everything out. Because if she didn't want me there, I wasn't going to stay there. The house didn't entirely belong to me anyway. The two of us had bought it ten years ago together. It is close to being paid off, which is the shitty thing about it.

"I guess we will know the answer to that when we get there."

We pass by the clubhouse, and I see there are already a number of motorcycles parked in the driveway. Everyone is waiting for my grand appearance.

Slash's house is directly beside the clubhouse. Slash's daughter Miley is sitting outside on the porch with ear buds in her ears. She has always loved listening to music for as long as I can remember. I wave at her when we pass by, and she waves back at me.

"How old is your daughter now?"

"She'll be eighteen in October."

Holy shit, I do not expect him to say that. Damn, she is older than what I expect her to be. It makes me feel old and I could only imagine how Slash feels.

"I bet she's boy crazy." I say it just to get Slash going. He is very protective of his daughter, since she now is an only child. "And I bet you're not liking that."

He grumbles when he speaks. "Don't even get me started with that shit; she's too young for a boyfriend. What she needs to do is focus on school so she can get a scholarship to college next year."

"I'm sure she'll get a scholarship to a good school." One that's probably far away from here. Slash wants her to get out and live her life. He doesn't want her to stay in Heartwood Springs forever. "She makes straight A's, doesn't she?"

He nods. "She hates me for making her study so much."

"But, in the long run, she will look back and thank you for it."

He pulls into my driveway, and I'm not surprised to see Natalie's tan SUV. She is the manager and owner of Heartwood Springs Diner, so she never schedules herself to work Fridays. "Don't do anything stupid. Get your shit and get out."

Why would he think I would do something stupid? The only thing I want to do is talk to Natalie. I have every right to do that.

I get out of the truck and walk up the porch's steps. The door to the house is already wide open. I glance around the living room and feel sick to my stomach. All of my shit is packed and sitting neatly on the floor.

Slash comes in behind me. "Let's get your stuff and leave."

I don't have a chance to respond because I hear someone walking around upstairs. Before Slash has a chance to grab ahold of me, I make my way upstairs. "Natalie, I need to talk to you!"

When I reach the top of the stairs, I hear laughter. The laughter is coming from a bedroom at the end of the hall. I open up the bedroom door and see a man naked on top of Natalie.

Anger surges through my veins and I tighten my fists. My nails cut into the rough patches of skin on my palm.

I was never getting back together with her now.

The guy gets off her and I get a good look at his face. He has big brown eyes and is bald. There's a scar on his left cheekbone and I know for a fact I've never seen him before.

Natalie has a smug little grin on her face. She is nothing but a fucking bitch for doing this to me. "I'm sorry, but I've got a new man now."

I want to wrap my hands around her neck and choke the life out of her. "You fucking bitch. You knew I was getting out of jail today."

Slash grips onto my shoulder, giving it a squeeze. "Calm down, brother. She's not worth it."

I lunge at Natalie but Slash holds me back. "Let me fucking go."

Slash's fingers dig into my skin, holding me in place. "I'm not letting you go until you promise me you aren't going to do anything stupid."

The guy who was on top of Natalie hurries out of the room and disappears out of sight.

Natalie still has a smirk on her face. "You need to get your things and go, because I don't want you here."

"This house is as much yours as it is mine," I spit out.

Slash loosens his grip on me. "You can talk about this some other time when you have a clear mind. The boys are waiting for you at the clubhouse, so let's get going and try to forget about this."

I don't know how I can forget about this because I thought she would change her mind. I thought the minute I got out of jail she would come crawling back into my arms. I didn't expect for her to have another man.

I try to get ahold of myself. "Alright then. Let's grab my stuff and get the hell out."

Natalie giggles when I go out the door. "See you later, Pete. We'll talk about the house some other time."

I can't believe I was with her for ten years, especially since she is nothing but a bitch and fucking whore.

# TWO
# CASH

MY CELL PHONE begins to ring as soon as I walk through the door of the bar. Much to my surprise, it's Slash. He hates using his cell phone and rarely calls me.

"Pete's with me now and will be staying at the clubhouse for the time being."

Natalie had broken up with him before he went to jail. I didn't think that the two of them would get back together. "It will be good to have him back."

"Natalie was in bed with another man when we walked through the door of their house."

I know just the person to occupy his bed tonight. "Bring him by the grill. I have someone that I want him to meet."

"We will be there in less than five. There's something else."

I hate to hear where this is going. "I hope that what you are getting ready to tell me is good news."

"Afraid not, brother. The man she was with is somebody I've never seen before."

Great. Someone new was in our town, and I couldn't

ask Sheriff Heath Evans anything about it until tomorrow. He was on vacation at Sweetheart Bay.

"We are definitely going to have to check him out later."

———

I turn my attention to Jaycee, who looks as tired as I feel. "So, how have things been today without Darcy?"

She shakes her head. "Things have been absolutely horrible, especially at lunch time. I'm glad that I get off in, like, five minutes. I don't think that I could have stood to work another shift today, even though Andrew asked me to."

It makes me angry that Andrew always turns to Jaycee to work. He doesn't give a damn about her not having a life other than this restaurant. She is one of the few people that works full time and will even work on her days off.

"I don't say I blame you for that." It is a Friday night, and she deserves to have some fun. Fun with Pete anyway. "You know, Pete got out of jail today. He's going to be here in a couple of minutes."

I've never seen her face light up so fast. Pete has been the only thing that she has talked about for months now. She was always asking about him, and now was the perfect time for them to hit it off. "I hope that Natalie is out of the picture."

"Oh, believe me, she will be out of the picture once you have your way with him."

She reaches across the table and gives me a hug. It's a good thing that Darcy isn't around or she would have socked her a good one. Darcy hates when women touch me. "Thank you for making my entire night. I don't know how I am going to repay you."

"The only thing that you need to worry about is showing Pete a good time." That was enough to repay me, because then Natalie wouldn't be in the picture anymore. I have never liked the bitch to begin with. I sure as hell didn't like her now for breaking his heart. "Don't you go worrying about anything else."

Slash and Pete walk through the door, and I get out of my seat to give Pete some brotherly love. "I sure am glad to see you again."

Pete has a big grin on his face. "I can't wait to see all of the boys. It sure is a good feeling being free."

It is nice to see that he was still in good spirits despite the circumstances.

Slash notices Jaycee sitting at the table. "I think that this pretty lady is waiting on you, Pete."

Jaycee cheeks turn red. "Would you guys like anything to eat or drink?"

I shake my head. "If I want something I'll go get it, Jaycee."

Slash shakes his head as well. "I'm good to go."

Pete is the one with the different answer. Jail food isn't all that great. "I'll take a cheeseburger with everything, french fries, and a pop if you don't mind."

Jaycee hops right out of her seat. "I don't mind one bit."

When she leaves, Pete's gaze goes directly towards her ass. This is a good sign, because I have no doubt in my mind he is getting lucky tonight. I just hope he doesn't break her heart, since she is a sweet woman.

"Why haven't I noticed her around here before?" Pete asks.

That was an easy answer. "Because you were too busy with Natalie."

A hint of anger flashes in Pete's eyes. "I can honestly say that I hate that fucking bitch."

Slash squeezes Pete's arm. "Easy now, brother. Don't you go thinking about her."

Jaycee comes back with Pete's soda. Her blue eyes twinkle and she tilts her head to the side. I haven't seen her this happy in a long time. "Your food will be out in just a few minutes."

Pete gives her a small smile. "Thank you, Jaycee. I appreciate it."

"Sit down with us and take a break," I say.

Jaycee glances around the restaurant. There are only about four tables that people are seated at, but other than that it's empty. "My feet are absolutely killing me today something awful."

She had worked a ten-hour shift today. "You be sure to enjoy your day off tomorrow."

Jaycee nods. "You don't have to tell me that twice."

Pete looks at Jaycee, who is now seated at the table beside him. "What do you say about coming to the clubhouse tonight? I could really use some company."

Jaycee's entire face is glowing. "I would love to. I just have to shower and change before I meet you over there."

Pete squeezes the inside of her thigh. "Just know that I'll be waiting on you."

Andrew yells at Jaycee from the kitchen. "Your order is up, Jaycee!"

Jaycee gets out of her seat and hurries off to get Pete's food. Pete leans out of his chair, cranking his neck to watch Jaycee's ass sway. I don't blame him for wanting some pussy because if I had just gotten out of jail I would want some to.

The second that Jaycee brings Pete's food to him, he

digs into it like he's never had anything to eat before. "I take it the food's good," I say, stating the obvious.

Pete talks with his mouth full. "I sure have missed this place."

Every weekend we would all sit down and eat here. Everyone came. There was no exception to that rule unless someone was out of town. It had been a ritual of ours for years, and I loved every minute of it. We could all catch up with one another and it gave us all a chance to talk.

"This place sure has missed you." Jaycee gets bold and rests her hand on his thigh. It was definitely on between the two of them tonight. "I know that I have sure missed seeing your cute self around."

I am trying my hardest to withhold my laughter. "Slash and I are going outside so that we can leave you two alone."

Slash hops right out of his chair as quick as he can. "I could really use a smoke break."

It would be good to let Pete and Jaycee have some time alone so they could talk privately. I need to have a conversation with Slash about Pete before I left to go back to the clubhouse. I hadn't gotten around to speaking to Andrew like I wanted to, but that could wait until tomorrow.

Outside, I am the first one to light a cigarette. "Pete seems calm and relaxed right now. I think Jaycee will keep his mind off of Natalie. At least I hope she will, because we don't need him going and doing something he will regret in the long run."

Slash seems to be thinking the same thing I am. "I don't see him doing anything crazy anymore, not with the girl around." He takes a puff off of his cigarette and blows out the smoke. "You sure did plan that out good, if I say so myself."

I make the work schedule every week and knew that Jaycee would be working today. "Let's just say I haven't heard her shut up about him in the last couple of months."

He laughs at my comment and shakes his head. "At least her fantasies are going to be coming true tonight."

I take several puffs off my cigarette before answering him. "I'm happy that I could help them in that department. To think, there is a stripper waiting on Pete at the clubhouse."

"I think Pete is going to like Jaycee so much better. He can look, touch, and feel her." Rather than with a stripper, he could only see her riding that pole. I still didn't regret the stripper because I knew the other guys would love it. "It makes me wish I wasn't so damn old, so I could stick around with all of you."

Slash is crazy for calling himself old, considering he's only thirty-eight.

"You should come over and enjoy yourself." I say it but know that he won't. He always comes up with a different excuse every time it comes to partying. At the end of the day, I just don't think he wants to party because of Miley being right at home.

"I better not. Miley is leaving with Nicole for the beach tomorrow. It will be the last time I have her in two weeks. I just want to make the most of the time that we have together tonight."

Slash only gets Miley on the weekends. It had been the arrangement that they had ever since their divorce several years ago.

I take a few more puffs off of my cigarette before putting it out. "If you change your mind, we would love for you to come over."

"I might come over if Miley goes somewhere." He

doesn't sound like he's thrilled with the idea of Miley leaving him, but she's not a little girl anymore. She loves hanging out with her friends and wasn't too fond of staying at home. "But I hope she doesn't. It seems like she never wants to spend time with old dad anymore."

"If she needs something from you, I'm sure she will come running."

Slash blows out smoke before putting his cigarette in the ashtray. "I know that all too well, because I give her everything she would ever want. I just can't not give her things because she's the only child I have left in this world."

He is the strongest person I know. Not only had he lost his son, but he has had so much bullshit in this life. My heart hurts for him and if a God did exist, I wish he would give him a break.

"I would do the exact same thing."

He goes quiet for several seconds, probably gathering his thoughts. "I guess I'm going to head back on inside now. We will meet you at the clubhouse in a little while."

"Slash, if you need to ever talk about anything, you just say the word."

He nods. "I might talk about things one day, but that day isn't going to be today."

We have had this conversation before, so I'm not surprised by his answer. I just hate for him to go through things all alone since he keeps everything bundled up inside.

———

When I get back to the clubhouse, the guys are all waiting outside for Pete's grand arrival. Martin already has a half empty bottle of liquor in his hand. Boy, he is getting started early. "Now if only Pete could get here so we could get this party started."

Bryce, the youngest member of the club at twenty-four, shakes his head in disapproval. "This asshole wanted me to get drunk and I don't like drinking."

"I say you just pick up a lady and enjoy your night," I reply.

There are more than enough ladies to go around if he really wants one.

A hint of a grin appears on Bryce's face. "It's been awhile since I've been laid."

"You should enjoy yourself tonight and forget that rule you have with not having one-night stands." I take out a cigarette and light it. "It would do you some good having a woman occupying your bed and having some fun."

Bryce seems to think about what I am saying for a minute, but shakes his head. "I don't know about that, man. I think I will stick to jacking off and watching porn."

Did he not want to eat some pussy and feel pretty fucking good?

I pat his shoulder. "You do whatever you want, Bryce."

Tommy slaps me hard on the shoulder. "It feels like it's been forever and a day since I have been here."

Tommy, the president of the charter in Sweetheart Bay, I have known my entire life. He is one of my best friends and always has our club's back.

"It has been a couple of weeks, that's for sure." He was due for a visit, and it was the perfect time to come. "I take it you are by yourself, since I don't hear Pam."

Pam, Tommy's old lady for the past twenty years, normally would come in to catch up with her only child, Martin. She keeps tabs on him like crazy. You would think he was a kid rather than a grown man.

Tommy chuckles. "Let's just say I wanted the luxury of seeing a stripper tonight. It reminds me of my younger days."

I blow out smoke and then shake my head. "Darcy would have me by the balls if I dared looked at one."

I didn't care much for strippers and hadn't ever since I had gotten together with Darcy.

"Don't tell Pam about me being here. I'll never hear the end of it from her."

At sixty, Tommy always tries to act like he's so much younger.

"I promise you, my lips are sealed on that matter."

My cell phone rings and I take it out of my pocket. "Hey, babe, I just wanted you to know that I made it," Darcy says.

"Are you sure you don't need me to come by and keep you company?" I figured the answer is no, but it doesn't hurt to ask. I am always constantly worrying to death about her.

"No. It's a girl's night, remember?" Of course, I remember. How could I forget about a night that means so much to her? "I'll see you in about an hour."

"I love you. Call me if you need anything."

"I will, babe. I love you too."

———

Tommy is still standing next to me, eavesdropping in on my conversation. "I take it that was Darcy. How has she been doing?"

"Working all the damn time. The restaurant is the place that she loves to be."

"I hope to talk to her later. It's been awhile since I've seen her."

When Tommy would come in, he normally left the next day. He has so many other things to worry about in his own charter back home. Since he doesn't stay long, when he comes in he rarely gets to see Darcy, or anyone else in the family besides the boys.

"She will be by later. You can talk to her then."

He gives me a hard, long look. "When are you going to propose to her, Cash? I know the two of you want kids. You're not getting any younger."

I don't pull out my ring and show him. Instead, I say, "Any day now, Tommy, any day."

THREE

## DARCY

IF THERE IS anything I hate in this world, it's being late. I had to stop by Heartwood Springs Credit Union to get money out of the bank to please Cash. He makes me pay with cash everywhere I go. It didn't help anything that today is Friday and the credit union was super busy.

Berkley is patiently waiting for me at a table we had reserved. I sit down across from her and let my blonde hair fall across my face. "I hope that you haven't been waiting long. I got held up at Heartwood Springs Credit Union."

Berkley lets out a sigh of relief. "You're fine. I'm just glad you're here."

I am glad to be here. I love my job and working for Cash, but I had to have a break. I have done nothing but work my ass off for the past six months. I should win the best girlfriend award because I will always work when Cash needs me to. Sometimes that would mean working ten straight days in a row.

Our waitress, Laken Head, comes over to where the two of us are sitting. She grins at us and I see her teeth are starting to rot out on top. I don't know for certain, but I think it's because of drugs. "What can I get you ladies to drink?"

"I'll take a water." I won't drink anything else. I have a figure to maintain.

"That's what I will have too."

Laken hurries off to get our drinks.

An icy chill prickles down my spine, and I glance around the restaurant, searching for the cause. My eyes land on Brody Jackson, a teacher at Heartwood Springs Elementary School, sitting with his daughter, Lynn. I don't see anyone else and I realize that I'm just being paranoid.

"How are things with you and Cash?" It's always the first thing she asks me if we haven't seen each other in a while. "Judging by that smile on your face, I take it that things are good between the two of you."

"I think he's going to propose soon."

Her brown eyes get big. "I don't know if I could say the same about Rich."

Berkley has been Rich's girlfriend for the past five years. She was indecisive with what she wanted to do with him, so she broke up with him all the time. Then the two of them would always find a way of getting back together.

"I love Cash and know that he's my one and only." I have known that about him ever since last year when I had lived with him. But he hadn't been ready to be in a relationship with me then. It was something I had to wait for him on. "I couldn't see my life without him in it."

Laken comes back and brings our drinks. "Shit, I can't believe I forgot to bring you menus."

Excellent customer service.

I don't need a menu. I want to eat something light tonight. "I just want a grilled chicken salad with ranch dressing."

"I'll take a cheeseburger and french fries."

Laken sets two straws down on the table. "I will be right back with your order."

After she disappears, I say, "Is it just me or does she look like she is on meth?" I like to gossip. It's always been in my DNA.

Berkley agrees with me. "I heard that she went to rehab not long ago."

It didn't surprise me, judging by the looks of her teeth, but she wasn't something I want to talk about anymore. I was dying to know about Berkley and Rich. "So what's the real reason you and Rich broke up?"

"I love Rich and I know that this sounds crazy." Berkley takes a sip of water. "But I'm afraid that he's going to land himself in prison for a hell of a lot longer than six months."

I understood her fear, but it wasn't something I thought about too much. I have been around the club ever since I was a little girl. I don't know all of the illegal shit they are all involved in. What I do know is that the guys are smart criminals.

"I don't think you should worry so much about things. Cash wouldn't dare send the club into murky waters. They know exactly what they are doing to stay out of trouble with the law."

"I guess you're right. I shouldn't be so worried about things." Berkley goes silent for several seconds and stares down at her hands. "I miscarried before Rich went to jail. He didn't even know that I was pregnant."

My eyes widen and I suck in a surprised gasp. "I can't believe you didn't tell me you were pregnant." I shake my head in disbelief. The two of us were best friends, or so I thought we were. She should have told me what happened so she wouldn't have had to go through it all alone. "You, of all people, should know I am capable of keeping a secret."

"It's just you have been so busy. I stopped by on the way to your house a couple of times, but you were never there."

"You should have reached out to me. I'm always around. If I'm not at home then I am at the clubhouse or working."

Her eyes gloss over and she presses her lips into a thin line. "I should have talked to you. I don't know if I'm going to get back together with Rich or not."

I couldn't believe what she was telling me. She was going to keep the fact she had a miscarriage from me on account of Rich. Why the fuck did that matter? Our friendship meant more to me than that. "Even if you don't get back together with him, you still have me." I reach across the table and squeeze her hand. "You sure as hell better not wait to tell me something like this ever again."

I bite down on my bottom lip and a tightness forms in my throat. She would be the first person I would turn to if I had a miscarriage. So why the hell wasn't I when it came to her?

I see Laken coming out of the kitchen with our food. Berkley's burger looks mouthwatering. The next time I come here I'm definitely getting a burger.

Laken sets our food down on the table. "Is there anything else I can help you ladies with?"

I shake my head and then glance at Berkley, who shakes her head also. "We're good for now," I say. "Thank you."

Laken looks relieved. "If that changes, just let me know. I'm going to go smoke."

Berkley nods. "Go ahead. You deserve it."

Laken cracks a smile. "You have no idea, Berkley."

After Laken disappears outside Berkley says, "I didn't mean to keep it a secret from you." She takes a quick bite of one of her french fries. "It's just that I feel like we haven't talked to each other in forever."

I feel the exact same way. Since Rich had gone to jail, she hasn't spent a lot of time at the clubhouse. Technically, she didn't need a reason to be around the club, even though the club treats her like family. I understand her reasoning for staying away, but that still wasn't a reason for the two of us not to talk.

"I'm glad that I saw you at the store on Monday." It was the first time we had spoken to each other in what seemed like forever. "If we hadn't had the run in, we would have never made plans for tonight."

"Tonight is just the thing that I needed. I have a lot on my mind."

I pour the ranch dressing on my salad and take a bite. The tomatoes, cucumbers, cheese, dressing, and spinach are absolutely delicious. It is just the thing I have been craving. "What are you going to do about Rich?"

She takes a bite of her cheeseburger before answering me. "At the end of the day, I want to get back together with him."

I sensed a big 'but' there.

"Can you live without him?" I ask the question of what things boil down to.

"I definitely could if I wanted to." I hate hearing her say that. It makes me believe she could walk away from him at any time. "But I don't think I will ever find a love like ours again."

I try to process what she's telling me.

"Would you mind elaborating on that?"

"I can definitely live without him, if I wanted." An unreadable expression forms on her face. "I know that he's always going to be there for me if I ever want to get back together. So I really don't have to think about living without him."

Rich considers her the love of his life and doesn't want anyone else. I didn't agree with how Berkley was so indecisive about him. It wasn't right for her to play with his heartstrings like that. Ultimately, he was her safety net because she knew he would always take her back.

"Leave it to you to make things complicated."

She picks at her fries like she's already full, even though she's barely eaten anything. "I wish things were more simple, but they're not."

Things weren't simple because she didn't want them to be.

I take another bite of my salad. "It's either you think he's your soulmate or you don't."

"I believe that we could have more than one soulmate in this lifetime."

She is my best friend, but boy, we didn't view things the same way.

"I love you, Berkley, but you're not right about that."

Her gaze wanders around the room and she slumps down in her chair. "The thing is, Darcy, I'm planning on leaving Heartwood Springs. I've never got the chance to experience life away from here. It's the biggest reason I want to let Rich go for good."

I jerk my head back and a lump forms in my throat. I wonder how long that she has been thinking about leaving. "I don't understand why you would want to leave after all this time. I can't imagine us not living minutes away from each other."

She shifts in her chair and pushes the food away with her hand. "I want you to move with me too. It's the chance for both of us to start over without being near the club. This club isn't good for either of us, Darcy. I think that you should leave Cash."

I jerk myself up from the chair, refusing to sit here another minute. "I'm going to the bathroom."

"I didn't mean to upset you, Darcy!" Berkley yells after me.

What did she expect for me to say? "I just need a few minutes to clear my head."

I walk past several empty tables and down the hall, disappearing from Berkley's view.

When I reach the women's bathroom, it's empty.

The bathroom door flies open behind me, slamming against the wall, and my breath catches in my throat. A man I don't recognize steps in, pointing a gun at my head. A swastika tattoo covers his hand. He inches closer.

I reach for my bag to grab my gun, but damnit I left my bag at the table. My heart slams against my chest and I level my gaze at the asshole.

"What do you want from me, you no good piece of shit?"

"You belong to Cash. We want to send the club a message." The gun is still trained on me and a devilish grin settles on his face. "The Southern Demons are back in town."

I spit in his face, not caring the consequences of my actions. "You are nothing but white trash."

His big hand reaches out, making contact with my face. Pain explodes in my cheek, radiating through my eye. "You better watch that mouth of yours, you fucking bitch."

I glare at him. "You go ahead and blow my brains out. I would like to see you try."

He wasn't going to kill me because that would be far too easy. What he was going to do was probably beat the living shit out of me. I hope that was all that he was going to do to me.He punches me in the stomach, knocking the breath out of me. "It's time to go, Darcy, so I suggest you start moving."

The asshole presses his gun into my back and silently urges me to walk out of the bathroom."Go up the stairs and don't even think about screaming," he whispers in my ear.

I go up the stairs to the apartment like I'm told. The pressure of the barrel doesn't lessen as I make my way up the stairs. The minute I reach the top of the stairs he pushes me into a bedroom door that's open.

I scan the room, my eyes landing on a video camera on the wall. I now see clearly why I felt like someone was watching me earlier, because someone was. That someone was a man who I don't recognize, a man that has a Southern Demons leather cut on. He is sitting at a table in the back of the restaurant, in the corner.

"Don't do anything to hurt Berkley," I say, pleading with him.

"That's the thing about it, Darcy. We didn't come here to harm Berkley." A wicked grin appears on his face. "We came here to kill you. You've always been the intended victim. It just so happens that Berkley came here with you."

Laken comes out of the bedroom and takes a good look at me. "You're a stupid fucking bitch, I'll give you that much. You've made this easy on the two of us."

I gape at her, my heart beating fast. An uneasiness settles against my stomach and my head starts to spin. This was something that they had planned out.

What did she have to gain for doing this to me?

"I've never done anything to you," I reply.

"The thing about it, Darcy, is that you have." Her eyes go completely black. "You walk around this town like you own the place! You and those fucking Reapers Wings don't allow any meth in this county. I have to travel an hour away just to get some. All of that is about to change, and I couldn't be happier about it."

Fear consumes me, but I won't let them see it. I glance around the room and realize that the only way out is the way I came in. I am absolutely fucked.

"This town has never belonged to me." The best thing I could do was try to reason with her. "Can you think about what you're saying for a minute? You and I both know drugs aren't good for you. The Reapers Wings keeping meth out of this county is the best thing that could have ever happened. I myself have never done anything physically to hurt you, because I don't find joy in hurting people."

The man clenches his jaw and paces around the room. "I've heard enough talk from the two of you."

Before I am able to do anything else, he hits me on the back of the head with his gun, knocking me unconscious.

# FOUR
# PETE

SLASH PULLS into the driveway of the clubhouse and everyone starts cheering. Now it was time to let the fun begin and get this party started. I step out of the truck, eager to greet every single one of my brothers. "I'm a free man now, boys."

Cash is the first one to greet me and he whispers in my ear, "I got you a little surprise waiting for you inside while you're waiting on Jaycee."

A grin appears on my face. There is nothing like seeing a woman dancing around a pole half naked. "Shit, I'm ready to have a fucking good time tonight."

"Go get them, brother, and don't worry about that fucking bitch tonight," Cash says.

I wouldn't dare worry about Natalie tonight when I will have another woman occupying my bed. "Believe me when I say that isn't something you have to worry about."

Tommy comes to me next and gets me in a headlock. "You're out of jail. You need to come visit me sometime."

I elbow Tommy in the gut and he loosens his grip. "It's nice to see you too, Tommy."

Tommy finally lets go of me. "I meant what I said about you coming to visit me sometime."

It would be nice to go to the beach for a weekend just to get away. "Depending on what's going on here, I should be able to go down there in a couple of weeks."

Tommy slaps me on the back. "You better or I'm going to whoop your ass for telling me otherwise."

Martin stumbles towards me, eyes glassed over, a big stupid smirk on his face. He plants a kiss on my forehead. "Come on, man. You're missing the party."

I follow Martin inside and walk over to the bar. There's a woman dancing around the pole and my heart hammers out of my chest. I catch a glimpse of her bare ass when she starts to dance. My erection throbs against me. Jaycee can't get here fast enough.

Hayden, a woman that isn't anyone's old lady, is behind the bar serving drinks. She has been around the club for the past decade.

Hayden takes one look at me and her lips curl up in a smile. "What can I help you with today, Pete?"

I don't want to be completely drunk and hammered when Jaycee gets here. I want to be able to feel something, instead of being numb inside. "I'll just take a beer."

Martin looks at me like I've lost my damn mind. "I want something a little stronger, like maybe a glass of whiskey."

Hayden opens up the bottle of beer and then hands it to me. "You are doing the opposite of what I would expect you to do."

I take a sip of the beer, enjoying every minute of how cold it is. I love how good that it tastes and could really get used to this. It's been five months since I have had a beer and, to me, that's far too long. "Yeah, well, I want to start slow so I can be able to remember this night."

Jaycee walks in the door and her entire face is glowing. To say she is a beautiful woman is an understatement. Her long brown hair is pulled up in a ponytail and she has the prettiest smile I've ever seen. Don't even get me started on how nice and round that ass is. Those breasts of hers are the perfect size and complement her slender shape. "I probably smell like greasy food. Where can I take a shower?"

I get up from behind the bar as Martin whistles after the two of us. "We can have the basement all to ourselves."

The basement is the perfect place to take Jaycee because it consists of a bedroom, bathroom, and sitting area. Things couldn't get any better than that and would give us a little bit of privacy at least.

Jaycee follows me down to the basement and when we reach the bottom, I am glad it is completely empty. Now it was time to let the fun begin.

I open up the door to the bathroom, my excitement growing stronger with each passing minute. "Look, Jaycee, I'm not going to lie and tell you I'm looking for an old lady. I am looking for just a fuck buddy for the time being, but that could change."

Her glow on her face doesn't change. It remains the same. "I never said that I wanted to be your old lady. I didn't even know you ended things with Natalie until Cash told me you had."

I don't want to hurt her, so I'm happy the two of us are on the same page. "I can assure you that Natalie and I are through. There is no way in hell I would ever go back to her."

She looks at my lips before saying. "Those words are the only words I need to hear."

I press my lips against hers, and she runs her fingers through my hair. She deepens the kiss and her tongue intertwines with my own. I run my hands along the front of her shirt and squeeze her breasts. Whimpers escape from her lips and it is a plea for me to do so much more.

"I'm sorry I never noticed you before." I trail my lips against her neck and suck on her skin. She runs her hands along my backside and stops at my ass. "It makes me feel like a piece of shit knowing the way you feel about me now."

She pulls off her shirt and then her bra, exposing her perfect little breasts. I have never known a woman to be so bold and sure of herself. This just made me want her so much more. "The last thing that you are is a piece of shit. You never noticed me before because you weren't single."

It still doesn't make me feel good knowing she had the hots for me when I hadn't paid her no mind. Tonight was going to make up for it because I was going to make her feel good and rock her entire world.

I press my lips against hers, silencing her. I undo the button on her blue jeans and she slides them down to her ankles. I slip my fingers inside of her panties, find her center mound, and then work them inside of her. Holy hell, she's already soaking wet for me, begging me for more.

"I can't say that I've ever fucked a woman down here in the clubhouse bathroom before."

She pulls down my jeans and sticks her hand in my boxers. "I can't even begin to tell you how long I've been waiting to do this to you."

I don't care how long she has been wanting to do this to me. I just want her to give me pleasure to help numb the pain. The last thing I want to feel tonight is anger with everything that has happened with Natalie. I want to feel alive inside, and feeling alive inside meant feeling fucking incredible.

"It's been so long that anyone has done this--" My words

die on my tongue and pleasure shoots through my veins as her lips slide down my penis.

She runs her tongue over the length of me and then looks at me with a smirk on her face. "How does this make you feel?"

"Keep going. Don't you dare think about fucking stopping."

She laughs. "I don't want to stop because I want you to feel good."

I am unable to say anything else because she has her lips on my penis again. This time her head is bobbing up and down as she takes the length of me in her mouth over and over. I let the rest of the world fade away and just concentrate on how she is making me feel fucking incredible.

"Fuck," I growl as I cum in her mouth.

She swallows me and then stares into my eyes. "What do you think about taking a shower now?"

I can't think of a better idea. "I don't have any clothes here. They are all in the back of Slash's truck."

Me getting my clothes from Slash hadn't crossed either one of our minds. I could always get them tomorrow.

She shrugs. "That's perfectly fine with me. I can just walk around naked."

Holy fucking shit, not only is she hot but I could stare at her naked all night long. I sure as hell don't plan on getting any sleep. Even when we weren't fucking, I planned on talking to her. I want to get to know her even if we are just going to be fuck buddies for now.

"We can wash your clothes so that you can have them to wear tomorrow."

She nods. "I might have to leave early tomorrow if they call me into work."

I don't even want to hear her already mention leaving. "Let's just enjoy ourselves tonight and worry about tomorrow when it comes."

She turns on the shower and then turns back around to face me. "I definitely like your way of thinking."

"I can't say that I always like my way of thinking. That's what ended my ass in jail in the first place."

She shimmies out of her panties and then steps underneath the shower. "I know Cash mentioned you went to jail for assault, but never did say much about it."

"Some guy was messing with my bike and it set me off. I decided it was a good idea to beat him up and paid the price for it."

"I can see how that set you off, as it would anyone else who works hard to keep their stuff nice and taken care of." I am starting to like her more with each passing minute. I wish I had paid more attention to her before. "I know how things are though, Pete, when it comes to jail and prison. It doesn't matter what you do. If we continue doing this, I will be always right here waiting for you."

I join her in the shower and press my lips against hers. She is saying and doing all of the right things to numb the pain. I enjoy talking to her because she doesn't judge me for who I am. "Thank you for being here with me tonight. You don't know just how much I've been longing for this."

Sure I was glad to be back with my brothers, but I wasn't really too interested in drinking. I just wanted someone outside of the club, particularly a lady that would listen to what I had to say. I wanted a woman that I could fuck and stay up with all night long, so that I could keep a clear head.

I run my hands across her breasts as the water trickles down on top of them. Her eyes close as soon as I touch her.

I'm rough when I fuck; I don't take things nice and slow. "You want to know what has always drawn me to you?"

She opens up her brown eyes and I could stare into them all day if given the chance.

I shake my head. "I can't say that I do."

"I noticed how unhappy you always were every time I saw you." She lathers shampoo in her hair and then I get underneath the water. The warm water feels amazing on my skin. "That unhappiness was something that broke my heart, because you were too handsome to be unhappy."

I can't recall a time when someone had said something so sweet to me before. But she was right about the unhappiness. The unhappiness didn't have anything to do with the club or my job at Heartwood Springs Auto. My unhappiness had everything in the world to do with Natalie, because she was so controlling. I had grown sick of her always trying to tell me I needed to be home at a certain time. I had also grown sick of us not having sex on a regular basis. It was like she had become an entirely different person.

"I want to know your story." I want more than anything to know more about her. I need to know more about her because I don't know anything. "I know you've got one. You are way too sweet to be single."

She moves back under the water to rinse the shampoo out of her hair. "I haven't been in a relationship with anyone because I've had my eye on you. You have been my crush for the past year and I'm not ashamed to say that."

"Are one-night stands something you do often?"

"I wouldn't dare have a one-night stand with any other guy at this point in my life."

Cash knew what he was doing when he had set the two

of us up. I was going to have to tell him tomorrow how much of a good time I was having with Jaycee.

There was something about her I was curious about. I had lived here my entire life and knew I hadn't ever seen her before until about a year ago. She's someone I would recognize, because she isn't a forgettable person.

"Do you mind if I ask you a question?" Just because we are going to be fuck buddies doesn't mean we couldn't talk and get to know each other.

She puts soap on a washcloth and then washes herself up. "You can ask me anything at all and I will answer it."

I already like that she is such an open book and doesn't have anything to hide.

"Why did you move here to Heartwood Springs?"

She laughs at my question and then shakes her head. "I thought you were going to ask me something personal." She sets the washcloth down and directs her full attention to me. "My grandfather Randy died of a heart attack and left me his house. The house is paid for and seemed hell of a lot better than paying rent in Sweetheart Bay. So I came here and have been here ever since."

"I'm sorry about your grandfather." I couldn't personally say I knew who her grandfather was, but I know that she misses him. "I hope you are here to stay, because I don't ever plan on leaving. This place will forever be home to me."

She runs her hands across my face and gazes into my eyes. "I don't ever plan on leaving Pete, not now or ever. That's not something you have to worry about. I love it here and would be crazy to leave when I've got such a good thing going."

That was the best thing I have heard all day. She is a sweet person and I might give her a chance.

"You do realize that you've made getting out of jail ten times better, right? I expected to spend the day with the guys getting drunk, but this, what we are doing, is so much better than that."

A grin appears on her face. "Thank you for giving me the chance."

I capture her lips with mine and rub my thumb against her nipple. "I want to be inside of you, Jaycee."

"Do it, Pete. You have no idea how long I have been waiting for this moment."

I press my erection inside of her and she moans against my lips, urging me to continue. I stare into her eyes as I empty myself inside of her. Natalie doesn't even cross my mind and this was what I was hoping for. It makes me feel more connected to her and much more enjoyable.

She stares intensely into my eyes. "Go faster, Pete. I promise you're not going to hurt me."

The shower is slick and I almost fall, so I pick her up and carry her into the bedroom, then sit her down on the bed. "You can tell me to stop if I become too rough with you."

"Don't be silly. Fuck me and fuck me hard."

I get in between her legs and take her the way that I want to. I start moving inside of her slow and then I pick up my pace. She works her hips along with me and arches her back as the two of us get into the rhythm.

I take her breast in my mouth and suck on her nipple. She runs her fingers through my hair and I go deeper inside of her. The two of us are so close to reaching the edge and I feel like my chest is about to explode.

A scream erupts from her lips, and her entire body goes still.

I run my hands across her face. "I don't plan on sleeping any tonight."

She kisses me hungrily and says, "Good, because I don't want you too."

FIVE
# ANDY

I DON'T WANT to be here in Heartwood Springs, because it's not my home. My home is and will always be in Texas. I love living in the city because there is so much to do. Living here in a small town means there's not much of anything to do. It takes an hour to get to the nearest mall and there's only one grocery store in town.

I long to be back in Texas, but I can't go back because of my husband, Hugh Jackson. I was forced to come here because of him. He may be my husband, but he is not a good man. My fear for what he would do to me if I were to leave him runs deep. It runs so deep I've stayed with him for the past year. I didn't know what kind of person he was when we got together. He was charming and sweet when we first met. Now he is nothing but a cold-hearted psychopath. I suppose his charming nature is how he won me over.

Hugh is in the living room talking to Hank when I walk into the kitchen to get a glass of water. It's the first time I have seen Hank the entire time we have been here. I wonder why he is here now.

Hugh paces around the room. "Liam is getting the job

done tonight and those Reapers Wings will never see what's coming."

I feel sick to my stomach. What has he gone and told Liam to do?

Hank chuckles. "I sure would pay money to see how frightened Darcy is. Did Liam tell you how he was going to kill her? I think I want dibs on her myself, since she's such a fine-looking woman."

"I don't give a damn how he kills her. He can even rape her for all I care; the only thing I'm concerned about is her being dead. She's the key to us sending a clear message to the Reapers Wings about us being back in town."

I have to get to the clubhouse to tell Cash everything that is going on. I would never be able to live with myself if something happened to Darcy. She had been my roommate when the two of us had lived in Texas.

"Where exactly are they keeping her? I might want to go see her later. I really want a piece of that ass before he kills her. Hell, I've been wanting that for years."

"Above the Heartwood Springs Diner," Hugh replies.

I grab the car keys that are on the kitchen table. I slowly open the door and then take off running for the car. I don't look back or think about what I have done. The minute I made the decision to warn Cash made it too late to turn around.

The door slams open, and Hank stalks toward the car, his face twisted in a scowl. I stab the key into the ignition just as Hank's hand is inches away from the passenger door.

I peel out of the driveway and floor it towards town limits. It will only take me about five minutes to get to the clubhouse. Five minutes that are going to take far too long. This is life or death here.

I run a light just as it turns red, narrowly escaping being

hit by a truck. Whoever is in the other vehicle lays on the horn. I don't care. I just keep on driving. I have to keep driving and won't stop until I get there.

I pass by several houses before I finally pull into the clubhouse. I can recognize Cash Daniels from anywhere. I have seen him a handful of times when he had come to visit Darcy. He was and is the definition of a gorgeous and unforgettable man.

His shaggy blonde hair and blue eyes are still the same. He's standing outside the clubhouse, smoking a cigarette. As soon as I pull into the driveway, his eyes fixate on the sports car I'm driving.

I hurry over to him gasping for air. "It's Darcy. They are going to kill her."

A puzzled look crosses Cash's face. "What the fuck are you talking about?"

"Hugh has put a direct hit on Darcy to announce that the Southern Demons are back in town."

Cash shakes his head like he doesn't believe anything I'm saying. "I don't fucking believe you. I don't know who you are. So you better start fucking talking."

"I was Darcy's roommate when she lived in Texas. I am Andy Knowles. Please, you have to believe me. We've got to go now."

He searches my eyes and looks me up and down. "Why would Hugh be here after all of this time?" It's more of a demand than a question.

"I'm sorry, but I can't tell you the answer to that."

"Is this some sort of joke?" He looks amused by what I am saying. "Because what you are saying is laughable. I talked to Darcy not long ago."

Why couldn't he just fucking believe me?! "Darcy is in trouble, and we have to go now before something horrible happens to her." I can only plead with him so much. "I honestly don't know why Hugh is back. He keeps me out of his business."

"You are full of nothing but shit."

My heart sinks, because whatever I say, there is no convincing him. I don't regret coming here. The only regret I have is that I won't be able to stop Darcy's murder. I tried and did my part, but it wasn't enough.

I nearly choke on my tears. The only thing I can see is Darcy lifeless in a pool of blood. I am going to have to live with that for the rest of my life. It is a tough pill to swallow that I had left for nothing. I can't go back to Hugh after what I had done. He'd have me killed. Now I don't know what I'm going to do. I have nowhere to go or hide. I'm nothing but a dead woman walking.

SIX

## DARCY

WHEN I OPEN up my eyes, my hands and feet are both bound. Pain throbs where the gun hit me in the head. I look around the room and begin to remember everything that had happened to me. Fear runs through my entire body and I wonder what the two of them are going to do to me.

Laken stares down at me with a grin plastered on her face. "It's a good thing you're finally awake, Darcy. You've been out for a pretty good while now."

"Why are you doing this to me?"

The guy who took me out of the bathroom is the one who speaks. "You, of all people, should know the answer to that."

It's then that it dawns on me. This has everything in the world to do with the club.

Tears stream down my face. I know with every single piece of my soul this is the end of my life. I wasn't going to be able to grow old with Cash and have our babies. "I don't play any part in anything that happens with the club."

"That's the thing about it, Darcy. You're Cash's old lady." Laken shakes her head in disgust. "What better way to send a message to the Reapers Wings than to let them know the Southern Demons are back in town? It's pretty fucking perfect if you ask me, isn't it, Liam?"

"I still don't understand why you're with the Southern Demons," I say.

"The Southern Demons have a lot to offer, Darcy, like job stability." Liam gives me a cold-hearted stare. It makes me wonder who he is and why he's here, since he's not wearing a leather cut. "Being in front of the camera, getting sexual pleasure, pays a hell of a lot of money."

I nearly barf in my mouth. Who in their right fucking mind would want to participate in doing sex tapes? It is the definition of sickening to me. "I take it that the Southern Demons also supply you with all of the fucking drugs you want."

"I really hope you don't have a problem with that." She sits down on the floor beside me and stares into my eyes. I didn't take her for someone who would get satisfaction from watching someone about to be murdered. "Because it will be over my dead body if that changes."

The door opens and Natalie comes in. A tightness forms in my chest and disbelief sets in. I have never had a problem or issue with her, even before she had ended things with Pete. "Andy left Hugh's house so the Reapers Wings now know Darcy is here."

I haven't seen Andy in years. It is nice knowing she still has my back. Now if only Cash could get here and take me home. He's coming, I know he is. I just hope he will come before it is too late.

Anger twists the features on Liam's face, and he draws his leg back, then slams his steel-toe boot into my ribs. Pain explodes in my side and a sob escapes my lips. "I can't believe this fucking shit, because this plan was supposed to work."

Laken yanks a pocket knife out of her pocket. She drops to her knees and presses the cold blade against my cheekbone. "I always thought you had a pretty little face."

A tremor runs down my spine, my body shaking at the thought of what they'll do next. "I hope you realize Cash is going to kill every single one of you."

The blade of the knife breaks through my skin. A scream rips from my throat. Hopefully someone, anyone, will hear me. "Oh Darcy, we are just getting started."

Natalie's beady eyes stare down at me, and a rotten tooth smirk cracks her lips. "How does it feel to know you are going to die today?"

Trembles of fear wrack my body, and I can only pray that Cash gets here in time. If he doesn't... No, I can't think about that. He will get here in time. He has to.

Hank strolls through the door. "You all have had your fun. Now it's my turn."

Hank grabs the back of my neck, and his foul whiskey breath assaults my nostrils as he lowers his dry lips to mine. He shoves his tongue in my mouth and I bite down hard. He's not going to violate me without suffering consequences. "You fucking bitch, you are going to have another thing coming for you."

Hank rears back and hits me in the cheek. Pain radiates through my face and then my cheek goes completely numb.

Liam puts a gun to my head. "Do you have any last words, Darcy?"

"Fuck every single one of you. I hope you rot in hell," I say bitterly.

My life flashes before my eyes, all the things I'll never be able to do. I will never be able to be a mother to Cash's children. It's the one thing in this world I've always wanted to be. The worst thing is knowing that I will never be able to grow old with Cash. We will never be able to have the wedding that we both want. All because of these pieces of shit.

Despite all of that, I have lived a good life. Not everyone can say that they have been in love and together with their soulmate in this lifetime. I am more than ready to meet my Maker.

The water escapes from my eyes as I think about all of the things I will be deprived of. I won't be able to have a family with Cash after all. The months that we have been together have been the best months of my life. I love him with all of my heart and always will.

A gasp comes out of my throat when he pulls the trigger.

The gun clicks and I start to believe I'm getting out of this alive. It gives me hope that God is on my side.

I have never seen someone look so outraged as Liam does right now. "I had this thing full of bullets earlier."

Natalie takes one look at me and then at Liam. "I can't have you shooting a gun in my restaurant. Berkley is still downstairs. Can't you just choke her or stab her to death?"

Laken still has the knife in her hand. "You don't have to tell me twice. All of you fuckers should have already let me do it to begin with. You're taking way too fucking long. I'm sure that Cash will be here any minute."

Hank shakes his head. "We just need to choke her to death. It will be fun watching the life escape from her. There's no blood involved, and it makes for an easy cleanup."

Liam and Hank both hold my feet down, making it impossible to move, then she situates herself on top of me.

Her hands are cool to the touch when she presses them against my neck.

There is only one good thing about dying. I will get to see my daddy again in Heaven. How I long to see him and will in just a couple of minutes. This will all be over soon.

Natalie plants her feet on the ground and shoves Laken out of the way.

Laken's eyes are bloodshot and she flares her nostrils. "What the fuck is this about?"

"You can't kill her," Natalie stutters on her words. "I have never had anything against Darcy. She's always been nice to me."

It feels good to know Natalie is on my side. At least one person in this room doesn't want me dead.

Liam hovers over top of me and pulls up my shirt, exposing my bra. Tears and sobs escape from my lips because my worst fear is about to come true. He is going to rape me and I can't do anything about it. "Let's have a little fun with her, Hank."

Hank slaps Natalie across the face. "You need to get the fuck out of here. I don't know why you even came in here to begin with."

Natalie takes out a gun from the dresser. "I came in here because I thought this is what I wanted, but I was wrong." She looks at Liam with a scowl on her face. "How the hell can you do this to her when the two of us are a thing?"

Liam gets off of me and glances at Natalie. "The question is why would you not want to do this to her? This is the definition of fun, if you ask me."

"I've had enough of this shit from you all." Laken takes out pills from her pocket. She grabs a cup sitting on the desk and smashes the pills. "I'm getting high if you idiots can't figure out what you want to do to her." She snorts the pills and smiles stupidly. "That's some good stuff right there. I wish that I had me some more."

Hank holds out his hands like he's done nothing wrong. "I'm just going to kill her so that we can get this over with."

Liam grabs the gun from Natalie's hands and hits her on the back of the head, knocking her unconscious. "Go ahead, Hank. I'll leave you with that pleasure."

Hank wraps his hands around my neck and within minutes I completely black out.

———

Light seeps through my eyelids, and the fog in my mind spirals around until it clears. Liam and Hank's voice filter in and out of my head. "She has been out for a good while. Is she dead?" Hank asks.

Liam's hand rests against my chest, probably feeling for a heartbeat. "She's still alive. Now it's time to finish her off."

Hank stomps towards the bathroom. "I've got to go take a shit. Those tacos I had earlier didn't settle well with my stomach."

My eyes flicker open when Hank leaves the room.

My eyes scan the room and stop on Natalie, who is standing in the doorway leading to the bathroom. She mouths, "I'm so sorry this was done to you."

Liam edges himself closer to me and I see the glint of the scissors in Natalie's hand. She creeps towards us, presses a finger to her lips, and then jabs the scissors in his collarbone. Blood oozes out of the wound and drips on the floor. "You shouldn't have done that, you fucking bitch. Now you're going to wish you were dead."

Natalie takes off, running farther into the apartment until she is no longer in sight. Liam runs after her and there is no doubt in my mind he's going to catch her. I don't know what he's going to do to her, but it's far from good.

Hank buttons up his pants when he comes back from the bathroom. "I guess I'll have to hold it since I'm the only one left when it comes to killing you. I didn't know how much of a pathetic person Natalie is. I would rape her a good time to see if that would straighten her up."

This is a bad dream I want to escape from.

His cell phone rings and he answers it. "Cash is on his way? Alright. I'll go down there to meet him since Brett had to leave."

Laken comes into the room and she stutters when she speaks. "What's going on? Why the hell isn't she dead?"

"Hold on, Hugh." He turns to Laken and shakes his head. "You could have killed her, but you're nothing but a fucking junkie. The only thing you like doing is getting high, and it's pretty fucking pathetic if you ask me."

I feel some sort of hope I am going to get out of this alive. Cash is coming to take me home and there is no doubt in my doubt he will get his revenge.

# SEVEN

# CASH

ANDY ISN'T LETTING up any time soon. "Would you fucking listen to me? I would not come here for no good reason. Darcy's life is on the line! Get that through your mind!"

My cell phone rings and panic sets in all over me, since it's Berkley. I haven't had a conversation with her since Rich went to jail. "I can't find Darcy anywhere." She sounds hysterical and worried. "She went to the bathroom about an hour ago and I haven't seen her since. I know she didn't leave because her purse is still sitting here and her car is still outside."

Rage rushes through me, sparking an inferno inside me. "Stay right there and don't move. Someone will be there soon."

Everything about Andy is coming back to me all at once. I remember who she is and I feel like an idiot for not believing her before. "Andy, where the fuck did they take her?" I remain as calm as I possibly can under the circumstances that I am in.

Tears stream down Andy's face. "I don't know. She's probably still at the restaurant."

My mind races and the only thing that makes sense is for Darcy to be in the apartment upstairs. "Andy, stay here and we will get you out of harm's way."

Andy nods. "Thank God you finally believed me."

I take out my cell phone and call Slash, who picks up on the first ring. "Hugh and the Southern Demons have taken Darcy." I bite back the tears that press against my lids, using anger to flush them dry. This was never supposed to happen. "I need you to come here."

"I'll be there in less than five."

———

Loud noise echoes through the clubhouse and I can barely hear myself think. I'm tempted to shoot off my gun to get everyone to scramble, but I don't. My eyes land on Bryce, who is at the bar talking to a petite blonde.

"Bryce, I need you to go outside and get ready to ride," I say, plain and simple.

Without a word, Bryce jumps up and heads outside.

I'm going to let Pete sit this one out. He needs tonight to get his mind off of that fucking bitch. I hope Jaycee is having the time of her life and he'll give her a chance.

Martin is probably in his bedroom by now. Tonight he wasn't going to get as much pussy as he was wanting. I need him tonight more than I have ever before.

I knock on Martin's door and don't get an answer. I wait several seconds before knocking again and still nothing. I open up the bedroom door and see Hayden naked on top of him. Her back is turned to me, so I see nothing but her bare ass. She gets off of him and looks at me with her mouth falling open.

"You don't have anything that I haven't seen before, sweetheart," I reassure her.

"What the fuck, Cash?" Martin clenches his jaw and fidgets with the blanket in his hands.

He'll get over it.

"I need you to ride." The tone in my voice is serious. "Next time, answer me if you don't want me to come barging in the fucking door. I'll be waiting for you outside."

I slam the door on my way out. Brian, the oldest member of the club, is hot on my heels, following me outside. Slash has probably already informed him of everything that's going on.

Slash gives me a hug as soon as he sees me. "She's going to be just fine."

The inferno inside me unleashes the demons that have been waiting to be let out. My demons are going to be unleashed tonight. I am on the brink of insanity and about to explode with what has happened to Darcy. It's the not knowing what has happened that fuels the flames.

My Darcy is the only woman who will have my heart. She's the only person in this world that understands a side of me no one else does. Not many women would want to get together with a man like me, much less stay.

In the time that we have been together, my walls have been broken down because of her. I let her love consume every single part of me. She gives me hope in this world in a way that no one else can. I love her more than life itself and my greatest fear is that she's already dead.

I nod. "I sure hope so."

Martin comes walking out the door and he looks more relaxed. "What's going on?"

"Hugh and his guys kidnapped Darcy." I'm glad that Slash says it because I don't want to.

"Everyone is with me except for Brian and Bryce," I say. Hugh has to know what is going on by now and Andy needs to get the hell out of here. "Brian, you and Bryce take Andy back to the cabin. The rest of you, we are heading out to Heartwood Springs Diner."

Andy sobs uncontrollably before the two of us depart ways. "I just hope that you get to her in time."

I hop onto my motorcycle and put on my helmet. "We're going to protect you and keep you safe."

———

The Heartwood Springs Diner has the closed sign on the door when we arrive. Berkley is sitting in a booth with a troubled expression on her face. "Do you mind telling me what's going on?"

"There's no time to explain everything." I turn to Martin, who stands behind me. "Take her to my house and don't even think about leaving."

Martin helps Berkley out of the booth. "Come on, let's go."

Berkley has a frown on her face but follows him out the door.

The minute that Berkley leaves, Hank comes out of where he is hiding in the bathroom hallway. "It's nice to see you again, Slash. I've been waiting for this day to come for the last couple of years."

Slash whispers in my ear. "Go see if Darcy is upstairs. I'll deal with this fucker."

I make my way towards the stairs, my anger getting the best of me. The ones who did this to her are going to pay, and I can't wait to get my revenge. The vein pulses out of my neck as I come undone. My greatest fear is standing before me. Darcy has to be alive or my heart will be in shackles. Shackles that will forever be locked and won't break free.

I open up the door and see Laken with her hands wrapped around Darcy's neck.

I get the gun out of my pants and point it at Laken's head. "You give me one fucking good reason not to blow your head off."

Liam lowers the gun and points it at my head. "I'll give you one good reason, because if that happens both of you are going to die today."

Natalie bites Liam's arm, and it brings blood. "Not on my watch they aren't."

The gun falls from Liam's hands, skittering across the scuffed hardwood. A loud bang reverberates through the room. An intense ringing in my ears nearly drops me to my knees.

Liam grabs ahold of his arm, wincing in pain. "I thought you learned your lesson before."

Laken tightens her grip around Darcy's neck. "Die, you fucking bitch."

I tackle Laken to the ground and slam her head on the hardwood floor. "I am going to enjoy killing you."

Darcy catches her breath. "Cash, please untie me. We have to get out of here."

Laken crawls towards the gun that Liam dropped, but I step on her fingers. The sounds of her bones crunching fill the air. Screams escape from her lips. "You're going to get what you deserve."

I hit Laken on the back of the head with my gun, knocking her unconscious.

Natalie grabs the gun and points it at Liam. "You two need to get out of here. The Southern Demons are coming."

I take the pocketknife out of my jeans and cut Darcy loose. My anger simmers down, and a wave of sadness washes over my body. I gather her in my arms and rub my hand across her cheek. "Oh, Darcy, I'm so sorry for what happened to you."

Darcy pulls down her shirt. I notice the shallow cut on one of her cheekbones. My eyes rest on her neck that is red from handprints. I don't even want to imagine what would have happened if I had gotten here a minute later.

Darcy speaks, her voice barely above a whisper. "We're not doing this right now. We can talk about this at the house."

I pick Darcy up in my arms and start walking down the stairs with her.

Slash is kicking the shit out of Hank when we reach the bottom of the stairs. "You are nothing but white trash."

Hank laughs. "You need to go back to Africa where you belong."

I grip onto Slash's shirt to hold him back. "He's just trying to get a reaction out of you, brother."

Slash spits in Hank's face. "I'm Spanish, you dumb ass."

"It's the same thing, if you ask me, because you don't belong here," Hank responds.

---

The minute we are outside, I hand Darcy her helmet. "Hold on tight, because this is going to be a rough ride back home."

I see the swarm of Southern Demons heading our way. Bullets come at us like we are soldiers at war.

Slash exchanges gunfire with them. "Cash, we need to

go, brother."

I start up my engine and pull out of the parking lot.

"How are you doing back there?" I ask.

"I haven't died today yet, so I would say that I am doing okay," Darcy answers.

The light turns yellow and Slash and I floor it. The light turns red before we get there, but we don't slow down. If anything, we go faster. We swerve around two coal trucks, putting the Southern Dreams behind them. The Southern Demons start heading in the opposite direction. They may be gone now, but they will be back.

————

I don't think I have ever been so happy to pull into my driveway as I am right now. I back up the motorcycle and then kill the engine.

Darcy is the very first thing I turn to.

"You're not going to talk about club business when we walk through those doors. Tonight I need to be in your arms, so don't plan on doing anything else. I need you more than I have ever needed you before."

Slash pulls in the driveway with a scowl on his face. "Those fuckers have got another thing coming for them, especially Hank."

I wrap my arms around Darcy to help her walk into the living room. The lights are already on, and when we step inside, Martin and Berkley are sitting on the couch. Martin plants a kiss on Darcy's forehead. "I love you, sis. Now go in there to get some rest."

Darcy bites down on her lip. "I'll see you tomorrow, Martin."

Berkley takes one look at Darcy. "What the fuck is

wrong with you, Darcy? How could you stand by Cash after what happened? Him and this club did this to you. It's beyond sickening. Rich and I are so through. You all are nothing but criminals. You're going to end up in prison where you belong."

"Don't even fucking start with this shit, Berkley." Darcy walks to the bedroom, but stops in the doorway. "This club life is all I've ever known. It's the only life I want. You don't disrespect any of these men in here. They are my family, and they would die for me if they had to."

Berkley has nothing but disgust on her face. "That's a fucking lie. You weren't around here for the past five years! You must not have liked it all that much or you wouldn't have left. I thought you would have enough sense to stay away from all of this, but I guess I was wrong. What kind of man lets their woman be beaten up for no good reason? Not a good one, I can tell you that."

My temper is rising with each passing second. "You don't know anything this club does, so I suggest you shut the fuck up. We are all family here and if you don't want to be with my brother anymore, then I suggest you fucking leave. If you leave, I can promise you won't have protection from any of us anymore and you're better off dead."

Berkley breaks down in tears. "Why did I get myself stuck in this situation to begin with?" she screams. Her guess is as good as mine.

Darcy takes one final look at her. "I'm glad that this was done to me and not you."

"It shouldn't have been done to anyone," Berkley replies.

Darcy slams the bedroom door shut behind her.

I need to talk to Martin before I can be alone with Darcy. "Do you mind staying with Nancy tonight?"

Nancy is just next door, so he does not have to go far. I don't think anything is going to happen. It will put my mind at ease knowing she is safe.

Martin nods. "I'll call you tomorrow morning."

I give Martin a hug. "Thank you. I'm sorry about earlier."

Martin shakes his head. "I should have answered you when you knocked on my door."

Slash looks at Berkley, who is sitting on the floor, then back at me. "What do you want me to do about her?"

I let out a sigh. "If she wants to leave, you're not obligated to protect her."

Berkley has a glare on her face. "Take me home, Slash, and I mean now."

Slash nods. "Go be with your old lady. She needs you more than we do."

I walk into my bedroom and shut the door behind me. Darcy is already in the bathroom sitting down in a chair. "I had a few things that I had to arrange. I'm sorry to have kept you waiting."

Tears are streaming down her face and sobs escape from her lips. "Laken, Liam, and Hank are the ones that did this to me. If it wasn't for Natalie, I would be dead."

I start running the bath water and make sure it's warm enough before turning to her. "Is Liam anyone that you've seen before?"

She shakes her head. "I would've been able to recognize him if I had."

"Is there anything else you need to tell me?" My heart breaks with each passing moment. "We can talk about this tomorrow morning if you don't want to discuss it now."

I was going to kill all three of them without any questions. I would find great joy in knowing they would meet their Maker because of me. It would do everything in the world to make my soul happy.

There is nothing but pain written on her face. "They didn't rape me. I thought I was going to die."

My chest tightens and my heart breaks in a million pieces, knowing all of the pain that she endured all because of me.

I turn off the bath water since the tub is full. "Let me help you get undressed."

She stands up from the chair and holds her arms above her head. I take off her shirt and my fingers trace the redness along her ribs. Her breathing becomes labored and she winces in pain. "I'm so sorry that you're going to be in pain tomorrow, sweetheart."

"I'm going to be just fine because you're going to be right by my side."

I unhook her bra and her breasts spill free. She slides the straps off of her arms and throws it down on the floor. I run my hands across her naked body and she closes her eyes. "You are the best thing that has ever happened to me and nothing about that will ever change."

She opens her eyes when I pull down her pants and underwear. "Nobody or nothing will ever break the bond I have with you."

I help her step out of the rest of her clothes. "You keep me from becoming a monster that I am so capable of becoming. Without you, Darcy, all my humanity would be gone. I love you with my entire heart and soul. You're the only good I have left in me."

She grabs ahold of my hand and lowers herself down in the bathtub. "Get naked. I need your arms around me."

I take off my shoes and then all of my clothes. I place my leather cut on the chair so that it doesn't get dirty. When I sink into the bathtub behind her, there is no hiding my erection. Just the sight of looking at her turns me on. I kiss the back of her neck and then wrap my arms around her.

"I can't even remember the last time we took a bath together. I could really get used to this."

She leans back against me and I kiss her hair. "I really want a baby, Cash. I know that it's something we haven't talked about a lot lately."

"Then we can kiss having these moments with each other goodbye." I say it as more of a joke than anything.

"I know we can make it work."

It's something I know we can make work too. I realize just how dead serious she is. "I'm on board with it if it's something that you want."

She turns around and gives me a peck on the lips. "It's something that I want more than anything in this world. I'm not getting any younger and you're not either."

I wrap my arms around her waist and draw her closer to me. A grimace forms on her face and I will do anything to take away her pain. "We will try to make a baby tonight, if that's something you want."

She doesn't give me an answer. Tears stream down her face. The pain and trauma of what had happened seeps out of her all at once. I am completely helpless and that's what hurts the most. I can only hold her in my arms and let her know I'm here.

Several minutes pass by and the two of us don't say anything. Words are something that are not needed. Me holding her in my arms as she breaks down in tears is enough. It's more than enough, because she's letting out the terror of what happened.

The trauma of what had happened will always be there. My hope is that over time the trauma will fade away. I have hope that it will because my Darcy isn't someone who could easily be broken.

"Please wash me up, Cash, so that we can get out."

I run the washcloth underneath the water and rub it gently across her face. The blood isn't caked on her face anymore and her cheeks are a shade of red. Staring back at me is the strongest woman that I know.

She stands up so I can wash the rest of her body. I am extra careful when I reach her ribs because they are dangerously red. It is going to take a couple of weeks for them to heal. The next couple of weeks are going to be painful, and I'm going to keep a close eye on her.

I get out of the bathtub and put a towel around my waist. "Do you need me to help you dry off, baby?"

She gets out of the bathtub and I wrap a towel around her body. "No. I can manage to do that."

I help her walk into the bedroom and put the bedsheets down. "What would you like for me to get you to wear?"

She dries off and then drops the towel to the floor. "I don't want any clothes. I just need you close to me."

"I'm going to go get you some Tylenol."

She nods. "I'll be waiting for you right here."

I leave the bedroom and shut the door behind me. The living room is completely empty and silence fills my home.

I get the Tylenol from the kitchen cabinet and a bottle of water from the fridge.

———

I hurry back into the bedroom and hand Darcy the water bottle and Tylenol. She swallows two pills down with the water. "I need you to make love to me, Cash, and to take the pain away."

I dry myself off and then stare into her eyes. "Are you sure about this?"

Making love is the last thing on my mind.

"I've never been more sure of anything in my entire life."

I hover over her and kiss her cheeks. Tears form in my eyes looking at her broken body but I hold them back. I am going to spend the rest of my life making up for everything that has happened to her. There has never been a time in my life I have been consumed with so much rage. This isn't something I'm going to come back from.

She reaches up and touches my face. "We are going to get past what happened tonight, and I don't ever want you blaming yourself. The minute we got together, I knew exactly what I was getting myself into. I mean it when I say it but there is no other life that I want than this life I have with you."

I press my lips against hers. "I'm glad to hear it, because there's no other woman in this world I would want to grow old with. There is no other woman that I would want to raise a family with but you."

She runs her hands through my hair, and I trail kisses down her body. I get between her legs and stick two fingers inside of her. Whimpers escape from her lips and I move my fingers inside of her faster until she is soaking wet.

Water escapes from her eyes and the only thing I can think about is taking the pain away."I need you inside me right now Cash."

I press my erection inside of her and then hold her gaze. "Let everything go and come to me, baby."

She closes her eyes and then several seconds later opens them up again. The sadness and pain pours out of her soul and into mine.

Our bodies move together in a perfect rhythm. My heart and soul are in flames as I stare down at her. She digs her fingernails into my back and I give every piece of my heart to her.

I kiss her neck where she is injured and then her ribs. The inferno takes over my body, my mind fills with their three bodies in the pits of Hell. "I promise you, I'm going to make this right tomorrow by killing every single one of them."

"I know that you will."

I move inside of her deeper and quicker until our bodies are united as one.

She wraps her arms around me tight, both of us breathing heavy.

I get ahold of my emotions when I lay down beside of her. "Nobody is ever to going to hurt you again."

"I know that they aren't, because I'm not going to let them." She sits up on her elbow so she's facing me. "My gun was in my purse and I didn't take my purse with me to the bathroom. I feel like the world's biggest idiot."

"You are far from an idiot, Darcy."

She makes herself comfortable in my arms. "I guess that if I would have used that gun, I wouldn't be alive right now."

I squeeze her tight with no intention of letting go. "I'm glad that you didn't have that gun with you, because I can't live without you." I would become a monster if something ever happens to her. A monster that is incapable of feeling anything like a human being. "You are the only thing in this world that holds me together."

She presses her lips against mine. "I'm the only thing that holds you together and you're the only thing that keeps me from falling apart."

# EIGHT

# ANDY

WE HAVEN'T MADE it out of Heartwood Springs when Bryce pulls into Heartwood Springs Auto. Before we had even gotten started Brian had mentioned that he needed gas. I have never been on the edge or frightened as much as I am now. Being in this county, out in the open, has my death written all over it.

I hop off of Bryce's motorcycle and look around me. There isn't a single soul in sight, and I wish we were already down the line. I don't even know where I am going because that's something they failed to mention. It's scary, living in the unknown, but that's how my life is going to be from here on out.

Bryce starts filling up his gas tank. "We shouldn't take long before we are back on the road. I promise this is the only stop we are going to make. We wouldn't have had to stop here if it wasn't for that old bastard."

Brian rolls his eyes. "It's not every day we have to help a damsel in distress. Excuse me for not feeling like filling up this week after the ten-hour work days I've had."

"Thank you for putting everything on hold to get me to

the cabin." Now life meant always being on the run. I have faith the Reapers Wings will always protect me and keep me safe. "I would be dead if I stayed here."

Brian shrugs. "You're not to the cabin yet, so you have nothing to thank us for."

That is true and makes the dangers of being here so much more apparent.

Bryce finishes filling up his motorcycle. "You want something to snack on, Andy?"

Going inside would do everything in the world to help steady my nerves.

"I'll just come inside with you," I reply.

Bryce puts his arm around me and the two of us make our way inside. "I'm warning you now that Brian is an old grouch, so don't take it personal."

I don't care about Brian being a grouch. The only thing I care about is getting to the cabin in one piece.

"Do you have any idea about where we are going?"

Bryce picks up a pack of mints. "The cabin we are going to isn't anything special. It's where Brian's older brother, John, lives."

Brian walks in the door and stares at the two of us. "You two going to be in here all damn night? We need to get the hell out of here before—"

I see the headlights before we come under fire. This is the exact thing I thought was going to happen. Hugh wasn't going to stop looking for me until he found me and killed me.

The gas station clerk stoops low and looks out the window. "I see three of them out there, so I can't say that the odds are against us."

"Andy, get down and stay away from the windows," Bryce demands.

My first thought is to lock myself in the bathroom, but I can't do that. The bathroom feels like it's a mile away from the car repair section of the gas station.

I can recognize Liam's voice from anywhere. "Give us Andy and we will let you go."

Not likely.

"You know that we're not going to do that." Brian sounds so calm and relaxed that I'm sure he's done this many times before. "Andy helped save Darcy's life because you pieces of shit tried to kill her."

Liam fires his gun at a window and the glass breaks. "I'm not going to tell you again. Give us the fucking girl. The girl is the only thing we are after."

I duck behind a candy rack, out of harm's way. My hands are sweaty and panic sets in. The last thing I want is to die today. I haven't done my fair share of living. "I'm so sorry that your life's in danger because of me."

Bryce blows off my comment like it's no big deal. "This is the fun part when it comes to being in this club. What are you talking about, girl?"

Worry sets in as I begin to wonder how we are going to get out of this situation. The last resort would be giving myself up, but that's only if none of us were to get out of this alive.

The gas station clerk looks through the window. "We've got to do something. They are bringing out the big guns."

The bullets riddle through the gas station and I nearly jump out of my skin. A water that had been sitting on the counter topples over and falls to the floor. A puddle of water forms on the floor and stops at my feet.

Bryce hurries over to the window, narrowly escaping a bullet. He closes one of his eyes and fires his gun. "I've got you, motherfucker."

Several seconds pass by and Liam begins to scream. "You killed my fucking brother!"

I can see it all unfolding before my eyes from the window.

Brian shoots Liam in the collarbone and that's when Hank urges him to leave.

"This is far from over!" Liam yells.

Bryce, Brian, and the gas station clerk all three fire their guns until they are out of sight.

Bryce sees that I am crying and comes over to me. "Andy, don't you go getting emotional on us now. Every single one of us is fine."

I couldn't help but feel emotional. What just now happened will be a never-ending thing. "Things shouldn't have to be like this. You shouldn't have to put your lives on the line because of me."

Bryce puts a comforting arm around my shoulder. "That's the way life has to be sometimes. It took a lot of courage for you coming to the clubhouse today. You're a hero for saving Darcy's life. You should be proud of yourself."

I will never consider myself a hero. Anyone sane would have done the exact same thing if their friend had been in trouble.

Brian interrupts our conversation. "Enough chatting. We need to get on the road. We've still got a good three hours left."

"A few of my buddies are coming by to help me clean everything up." The gas station clerk looks directly at Brian. "I am going to shut everything down before they get here."

Brian squeezes the man's shoulder. "It's a good thing you're cleaning up this mess, because I sure as hell don't want to."

The three hours on the back of Bryce's motorcycle are the longest three hours of my life. When he pulls into a long winding driveway in North Carolina, relief washes over me. Now to try to get some rest tonight because we are heading into Sweetheart Bay tomorrow.

Brian told me before we left Heartwood Springs about us going to Sweetheart Bay. His reasoning behind it is because the club there would be able to take better care of me. He said that Tommy's crew in Sweetheart Bay has sixteen members, and that's double from the club in Heartwood Springs.

"You're not asleep on me, are you?" Bryce asks.

How the hell could I have fallen asleep after everything that had happened?

"No. I'm just glad nobody followed us down here."

"That makes you and me both." Bryce parks his motorcycle in the driveway. "Now we just need to make it in the house in one piece. I wouldn't want to scare you by weaving between cars."

Brian is the first one up to the door of the house. The sounds of a dog barking can be heard from inside. "It's a good thing I called my brother when we were back at Heartwood Springs so he could put that damn dog up. That damn thing will attack you as soon as you walk in the door."

John opens the door and ushers us inside. His hair is white and wrinkles are on his cheeks. He looks to be seventy, maybe eighty. "Come on in now. I'll show you where you're going to sleep."

I don't want to sleep alone. I couldn't sleep alone or I would never be able to get any sleep. The fear would set in as soon as my head hit the pillow. The nightmare that is my life would come pouring out in my sleep. I didn't want to be alone or scared if that would happen. I want someone laying beside me.

John leads us down the hall and into a small bedroom. There isn't anything special about it. The bedroom doesn't have any pictures or furniture; the only thing it has is a bed. "You can sleep in here, Andy."

I grab hold of Bryce's arm before he leaves. "Will you stay in here with me?" The desperation not to be alone comes out in my voice.

Bryce looks at me nervously. "Sure. I guess I can."

John stops walking down the hall and looks Bryce right in the eye. "That's good that you're staying in here, because you would be sleeping on the couch."

Bryce shrugs. "I don't have a problem with that either way."

Brian rolls his eyes. "If you would have gotten rid of that damn dog, we wouldn't have that problem."

John ignores his comment. "That dog keeps me from going crazy. It's not very fun being all alone out here."

The last thing I hear is Brian grumbling. "You should have kept your wife happy and she wouldn't have left you. Now you have that damn dog to feed and take care of. If it was me, I would much rather be alone instead of spending my money on some damn dog. But I guess it's a good thing you're not me, isn't it?"

For the first time today, I crack a smile. I could listen to them talk all day and don't think I'd ever get tired of it. "They sure do act like siblings."

"Yeah, they do. I've seen John a couple of times in Heartwood Springs but not much. I really can't say I know much about him though, other than the fact he's not a member of this club anymore. I think arthritis got the best of him."

"I would hate being out here all alone. It would give me the creeps, since we are so far away from everybody and everything."

"That's the thing about it, Andy, you don't have to worry about being all alone out here." Bryce sits down on the bed and looks at me, uneasy. "The Reapers Wings are always going to keep you safe."

"I know that you are. I would be dead right now if it wasn't for all of you." I can't get over how he's staring around the room, searching for an escape. "Is something wrong?"

"I'm not a one-night stand type of guy and don't plan on having sex with you."

I think what he says is hysterical and I crack up laughing. It takes several seconds to get ahold of myself before I can speak. "I wasn't planning on having sex with you, Bryce. I'm not a woman who has one-night stands either."

"You had me worried for a second there, because I thought that's what you wanted."

He sure does seem awful sweet.

"I just didn't want to be alone tonight."

"I can't say that I blame you." He gives me an understanding nod. "It seems like at night all hell breaks loose with things going on in inside my mind."

"I guess the things you are talking about are from the club."

He shakes his head. "This club has nothing to do with my fucked-up mind." So I did assume wrong. "Spending six months in Iraq and seeing my best friend being blown up caused that."

It makes sense, him being a veteran, especially the way he had killed that guy back there. "I know that saying *I'm sorry* doesn't help anything. But I truly am sorry you had to witness something so terrible."

"Thank you. You're the first person I've told that to."

That has to feel good to get that off of his chest.

"You should tell the boys. I'm sure they would understand."

He takes off his boots and then lays back against the bed. "I have no doubt in my mind that they would. I just don't like putting myself out there. I'm used to being alone and keeping my mouth shut."

"Sometimes it pays off to talk. If I wouldn't have today, Darcy wouldn't still be here."

He looks at me with confusion. I don't think he realizes everything that is going on. The guys probably hadn't had a chance to talk to him about everything. "Do you mind catching me up on what happened?"

I don't know everything, but I tell him what I do know. "Hugh has beef with the club and wanted to kill Darcy. He knows that she is one of the most precious things to Cash. I found out his plans and stopped him from following through with them."

He folds his arms across his chest, a distant look on his face. "That is some of the deepest shit I've heard in a long time. I guess that things will never go back to the way they used to be."

I was sure that it changed a hell of a lot of things. But there wasn't anything else I could do about it. I had done my part in telling Cash about Hugh's plans.

"It changes everything and has caused an all-out war."

"I wasn't able to function in everyday society after what happened to me in Iraq. I felt like an outcast and I met Cash at the bar he owns. He took me under his wing and introduced me to the club. The rest is history because I found a place where I belonged and that's with the Reapers Wings."

"How long have you been a member?"

"Only a year, but that year has been amazing."

That makes me happy to hear him say that. I don't understand why people give outlaws a bad rep. Not all of them are psychopaths or crazies – a majority of them are good people.

"Do you have a girlfriend?" I ask him the one question that is lingering on my mind.

"I was in love once and she broke my heart. Ever since then, I've been single. I can't really say I want a woman in my life right now." I don't like where this story is going. It seems like his life has been filled with nothing but pain. But he is still a super sweet guy. "I proposed to her when the two of us were only teenagers, but she wouldn't marry me. She didn't want to be tied down at such a young age."

"You can't blame her for not marrying you if the two of you were too young."

"I *don't* blame her for not marrying me." He doesn't seem the least bit bothered by what I said just now. I really enjoy talking to him and will miss him. "I still can't stop thinking about her after all of this time. It's the reason I won't have one-night stands. I'm not quite over her and not sure if I ever will be."

I lay down in bed and wrap the covers around me. "Maybe you should try to get in contact with her."

He gets up and turns off the light, making it pitch black. "I don't do social media, so that's not going to work."

He is just trying to complicate things. It would be simple for him to look her up on social media and get in contact with her. Getting in touch with her would do everything in the world to give him peace of mind. "I don't know what to tell you, Bryce."

He climbs back into bed and faces away from me. "I just need to let her go."

I don't think that letting her go is such a good idea. Chances are, if he is thinking about her all the time, there is a possibility of her thinking about him too.

"Then if she walks back in your life, you'll start that entire process over again."

He lets out a loud sigh. "Thanks. You're real helpful."

"What can I say? I try to be."

"Good night, Andy."

"Can you put your arms around me?" I normally don't cuddle, but there is just something about him.

He turns back around and gets himself situated. "Alright, then. Come over here."

I know he isn't going to try to put any moves on me. I rest my head against his chest and he wraps his arms around me. For the first time in a long time, I feel safe and secure. I have hope that nothing bad is going to happen to me.

"Thank you for sleeping in here with me tonight. It does everything in the world to give me peace of mind."

"There is no need to thank me, Andy." He kisses my forehead. "I'm just doing my part in keeping you safe."

# NINE

# PETE

JAYCEE IS ASLEEP BESIDE ME, and I'm careful when I get out of bed not to wake her. It's past two in the morning, but I can't sleep. The only thing I can think about is that guy who was on top of Natalie, naked. I can't help that it makes me angry. It's an image I can't shake off.

I put on the shorts and t-shirt I found in the dryer, then make my way upstairs. The party is still going strong because we know how to party. A few people are passed out cold on the couches and beer cans are on the floor.

I get a beer out of the fridge and then sit down at the bar. Tommy sees me the minute I sit down and joins me. I don't see the rest of the boys from the club anywhere and that alarms me. Surely they couldn't be asleep already.

I smell beer on Tommy's breath when he speaks. "The Southern Demons beat Darcy, so everyone headed out earlier."

I open up my beer and take a swig. "Shit, they could have told me about it and I could have helped out."

"They aren't doing nothing else tonight. Cash is staying with Darcy." I couldn't think of anything worse that could have happened. The Southern Demons left ten years ago and now they were back, ready to finish the war they had started. A war that did not truly end. "I'm calling my chapter in Sweetheart Bay first thing tomorrow morning and sending three of my guys down here. We are going to need all of the help we can get, because Darcy had three attackers."

Holy fucking shit.

"I hate that about her, I really do." This is just the beginning of all hell breaking loose. "It doesn't surprise me that something happened. Things have been too peaceful here in this county. We've all gotten too comfortable with how things have been around here and let our guards down."

"Those Southern Demons have me worried about my charter in Sweetheart Bay. We have had no trouble out of them so far. It's enough for me to realize that we need to watch our backs. It will only be a matter of time before they make their presence known in Sweetheart Bay."

It has me curious why they would come back all of a sudden. There has to be a bigger reason than them wanting to claim our territory as their own.

"What makes you say that?"

"I have a feeling they want to bring drugs in on the north side, because they won't have any competition. It will be a perfect setup for them to run a pipeline through there, but we aren't going to let them."

I finish off my beer and get another out of the fridge. "All of us are going to have a lot on our plate."

"You have got that right. All it does is add stress to everything else that is going on."

I wonder what stress he is talking about, but don't have a chance to say anything. Jaycee is walking our way, wearing her clothes from earlier. I had put them in the washer and dryer for her before we laid down.

A guy I don't know comes up behind Jaycee and grabs her ass. "I haven't seen you all night. Where have you been hiding?"

Jaycee has a horrified expression on her face. "I haven't been hiding anywhere. I don't appreciate you grabbing my ass."

I get up off of the bar stool and shove the guy. "Jaycee is with me, so I would suggest you keep your hands off of her."

What I say doesn't appear to faze him. "The three of us should have a threesome. She's much too pretty for you to have her for yourself."

My fist hits his nose, bringing the blood. "We aren't having a threesome with you, you nasty piece of shit."

Jaycee grabs hold of my arm, holding me back. "I'm fine, Pete. You got your point across. Just forget about him."

Tommy takes his gun out and fires it in the air. The music stops playing and everybody stops what they are doing to stare at him. "This party is over. Everyone needs to go back home."

People trample over beer cans and shove each other out of the way to get to the door. It's amazing the things people will do when a gun is fired.

The man glares at me on his way out. "You better hope I don't see you around town, Pete. This is far from over."

I flip him off. "I'm not in the least bit scared of you."

"I'm going outside to see if that asshole does anything to our bikes and then going to bed," Tommy tells me. "You should rest up, Pete. We've got a long day ahead of us."

Jaycee sits down on the couch that is now empty. "I'm sorry for coming up here. You got out of bed and I didn't want to be alone."

"Don't be sorry, Jaycee. It's perfectly alright." I kiss her cheek. "You want a beer or something to drink?"

She shakes her head. "I think the two of us should talk."

I don't know where she is going with this. The last thing I'm going to do is tell her how I have been thinking about Natalie. "What is it you want to talk about?"

Tommy walks back in the door and heads towards his bedroom. "Good night."

"Good night," Jaycee and I both say.

"I'm sorry about what happened back there."

"That guy got what he deserved."

It's nice to know me punching that guy's lights out doesn't make her angry or upset with me. "I thought maybe I scared you for a minute there with how I reacted."

She grabs hold of my hand. "You punched that guy for grabbing my ass. It's the sweetest thing anyone has ever done for me."

I let her lead the way back down to the basement. "Any guy would be crazy to have not done the same thing."

When we reach the bedroom, she kisses my lips. "For you being so sweet, you get a reward."

I love where she is going with this. "What's my reward?"

She puts her hand in my shorts and run her hands across my penis. "That's something you're just going to have to guess."

I pull down my shorts to give her better access. "I sure as hell hope you would never want to have a threesome."

She gets down on her knees. "No, I would never want a threesome. I need you all to myself."

———

The next morning, Jaycee yawns before getting out of bed. "I have got to get going. I need to feed my cat, Precious."

I didn't think she would leave so soon. "I didn't know that you have a cat."

She gives me a quick kiss and then smiles. "Because you didn't ask me if I have a cat, silly."

I put on my boxers and follow her up the stairs. "What do you say about staying for some breakfast?"

Her eyes have dark circles underneath them and her hair is disheveled. "I'm going to crash when I get back home. Thank you, though."

The two of us make our way outdoors where Tommy is polishing up his bike. "I hope that I didn't scare you shooting off that gun last night."

She laughs. "You didn't scare me, Tommy. I'm no stranger to hearing guns being fired."

I give her one final goodbye kiss. "What are you doing later?"

"Having supper with you at seven, so don't be late," she answers.

I open her car door and she gets in. "Do you live out by Bear Den Road?"

She starts the car. "I do."

"I'll see you then," I say.

Her face lights up.. "I'm already looking forward to it."

I watch her car until it disappears out of sight.

Tommy punches me hard in the arm, knocking me out of my trance.

I rub my arm with my hand, because it stings. "What the fuck is that for?"

"Being stupid and punching that guy last night."

The guy was lucky I hadn't done anything else to him.

A black SUV pulls into the driveway and Tommy gets

his gun out. This definitely has Southern Demons written all over it, with the tinted windows and nice rims. "I wonder what the fuck they want."

"I don't know, Tommy. Why don't you go ask them?"

Tommy smirks. "Nice comment, smart ass."

Natalie gets out of the passenger side of the SUV and then the SUV floors it quickly out of the driveway. I wonder why the fuck she is here. It mostly definitely isn't for me, because she has broken up with me.

"I'm here to get the car Andy parked here." Natalie's face is a mixture of black and blue. It makes me wonder what happened to her, not that I give a shit about it. She moves towards me with a frown on her face. Her chin trembles when she speaks, her lips quivering. "I regret breaking up with you, Pete. I was wondering if the two of us could talk."

I will never be able to shake the guy being naked on top of her. My anger simmers beneath the surface and I feel like I'm about to blow. The only reason she wants to get back together with me is because, I assume, someone slapped her around. "I haven't got nothing to talk to you about. You are nothing but a fucking bitch for doing what you did to me yesterday. I guess that it's not convenient for you to be together with him anymore, since he gave you a beating."

She tries to reach out and touch me, but I back away from her. "You can't blame me for the things that happened while you were locked up."

The rage that consumes my body is dying to be let out. "We aren't having this conversation right now. You need to fucking leave."

She looks unhappy and there isn't a damn thing I can do about that. "The Southern Demons are back in town and are going to control this town if you let them."

"I guess that guy you were fucking is a Southern Demons." I lose all control of myself and tackle her to the ground. She deserves to be in the fiery pits of hell. I want her to be fucking scared of me. It fills me with nothing but pleasure knowing that she is terrified. The fear is in her eyes and my demons are about to be unleashed. "You know we hate their fucking guts!"

Tommy grabs hold of me and puts me in a chokehold before I can wrap my hands around her throat. It is too bad Tommy is here. If he wasn't, I could let all of my demons come pouring out of my soul.

"I would suggest you get the fuck out of here before I kill you myself!" Tommy yells.

Natalie hurries over to the sports car and gets in. "Don't say I didn't warn all of you, Pete. I'm so sorry about what happened to Darcy."

Tommy loosens his grip on me when she pulls out of the driveway seconds later. "What the fuck was that about? You must be crazy to do that shit. Damn, I thought you was going to kill her."

He finally lets go of me and I'm able to catch my breath. "I caught her in bed with another man yesterday."

"I can see your reasoning, but you're not going to kill her today. Not while I'm here." Tommy puts on his helmet and starts up his motorcycle. "Now let's go riding so you can have a clear head and get rid of some of that rage."

TEN

## ANDY

THE NEXT MORNING I wake up to the bed being empty beside me. Bryce must have been quiet when he had gotten out of bed, because he didn't wake me.

I get out of bed and walk past the bathroom, where I hear the shower going. The bathroom was probably where Bryce had escaped to. A shower seems nice right about now. I look down at my old tank top, filled with holes. My jeans aren't much better because they are so tight. I hope that when I get to Sweetheart Bay someone will buy me new clothes. I desperately need them.

John is in the kitchen, making biscuits and gravy. "I was hoping you would get up soon, so you could have some breakfast before you all hit the road. I take it you slept okay."

"Thank you for making breakfast. I can't say I know when I'm going to be having a meal again."

It probably won't be any time soon. Brian seems dead set in getting to Sweetheart Bay. I don't think he'll stop before the three of us get there, but I could be wrong.

John gets the biscuits out of the oven. "No reason to

thank me. I have been wanting gravy for a while now. Now is a good time as ever since I finally have guests."

By the sounds of it, he must not get a lot of visitors on a daily basis. I hate to think that he spends most of his time alone. To me, it would be boring living by myself. It would drive me up the wall.

"You don't have any grandkids or anyone that comes to visit you often?"

He hands me a paper plate and fork so that I can make a plate of food. "My kids and grandkids don't live close by. They are all scattered out everywhere and not one of them volunteers to check in on me."

"I am sorry to hear that." I set two biscuits on my paper plate, then pour the gravy on top of it. "To me, that doesn't seem right or fair. Surely you talk to them on the phone though, don't you?"

"I'll be the first to tell you that there's a difference between talking to someone on the phone and seeing them in person."

The plate of food nearly burns my hands and I set it down on the table. "Well, just know when this all blows over, I'll come back up with Brian. I'm sure he comes up and visits you sometimes, doesn't he?"

He laughs like what I say is almost comical. "This is the first time that I've seen Brian in a year. But I do go to Heartwood Springs and stay a few days during the holidays. I can't be gone long though. Brian won't let me bring my dog when I stay with him."

Bryce comes into the kitchen. His brown hair is wet from the shower. The scent of soap and masculinity surrounds me as he stops over by the food. "Damn, that food smells and looks good. I'm absolutely starving."

John sits down at the table with his cup of coffee. "Go

ahead, help yourself. I know very well that Brian isn't going to stop anywhere for a couple of hours. He might just go straight through when you all go home."

Bryce looks at John like he's crazy. "I can't say I agree with that. I don't like going without eating or it makes my head hurt. I become the world's biggest asshole, which isn't a side of me anyone needs to see."

I can't imagine seeing him that way, considering how nice he has been towards me. "Why is Brian in such a rush to get to Heartwood Springs?"

John takes a sip of his coffee before answering. "He wants to see how much damage has been done to the shop after what happened last night."

"Where is Brian at anyway?" I figured it would be just a matter of minutes before we got the show on the road.

"Outside, sitting on the porch, talking to his daughter on the phone. His daughter is the reason he works all the damn time. He pays all her bills so she can finish school. She's thirty-four and never comes in to see him, but takes his money. I can tell you right now I wouldn't do that for nobody, especially if they couldn't come around. It's the reason why my own family won't come to see me."

I don't blame John for that, though I don't know the entire situation. It seems pretty crappy. "I can see why you got your dog. You must be lonely up here all alone."

John nods. "It's just too bad my dog can't talk to me and that I can't have a conversation with him."

Bryce finishes off his plate, then gets up to make himself another plate. "I can't even begin to tell you the last time I had biscuits and gravy. I am more of a cereal every morning kind of man, since I can't cook worth shit."

John laughs. "Cereal every morning gets old after a while, no matter if you switch up the brands."

I take a small bite of the biscuits and gravy, and it's every bit as delicious as Bryce claims it to be. "I hope when we get to Sweetheart Bay, whoever is staying with me will make a run to the store and pick up some food. There is no way I'm eating cereal every day."

Brian walks in the door with an annoyed expression on his face. "She wants me to send her three thousand dollars, and I told her I didn't have that kind of money right now. So guess what she does? Hangs up on me."

"Get yourself something to eat and don't worry yourself sick over Leah. She's grown," John says, but I know Brian is going to worry about her just the same. "You shouldn't have been sending her money all of these years, anyway."

Brian makes himself a plate of food. "Yeah, but this time around I'm going to be a grandfather again."

"You've got yourself in a mess, Brian. You'll be working until you are dead," John says before getting up from the table.

Brian has a scowl on his face and I myself was sorry that I have been one of the reasons for that. "Andy, we are going to be leaving in the next hour or so, then you'll be with the guys at Sweetheart Bay."

"I'm sorry that you had to bring me here," I say.

Brian takes a bite of his food before answering me. "I'm not. I have had a nice visit with my brother."

I hear John's dog barking and I rub the back of my neck. What if someone else is here? Knots form in my stomach at the thoughts of having a replay of last night. I just want to be out of harm's way. Nothing can happen to these men because of me.

John sees the look on my face. "He's just got to go outside and use the bathroom, Andy. Everything is alright."

The fear comes out in my voice. "After what happened

last night, I am worried that they are going to come looking for me."

John shows me the gun hidden underneath his shirt. "You've got nothing in this world to worry about. I may be an old man, but I know how to protect myself."

Brian doesn't look at all worried. "Andy, if someone comes up here looking for you, we're going to keep you safe."

John leaves the room to let his dog out of the bedroom. John's dog comes into the living room with his tail wagging. His ears are droopy and he's smiling back at me. He doesn't look the least bit mean like Brian mentioned.

"What's the dog's name?" I ask.

Brian rolls his eyes. "Baby."

John opens up the door to let Baby out and then hurries after him.

I watch the two of them from the window and laugh. John bends down to pet Baby and Baby licks his face.

Bryce gets up from the table. "It's been forever since I've been able to pet a friendly dog.'"

Brian finishes off his plate. "Go ahead and spend time with that damn dog, Bryce. If it bites, don't come crying to me."

Bryce doesn't pay his comment any mind. "I've been wanting me a dog for a while now. Maybe I will get me one soon."

I watch Bryce talking to John from the window, and Baby is wagging his tail.

"Andy, I don't mean to rush you, but now is a good time to get going." Brian stands up from the table and stretches out his legs. "We have a long day ahead of us and Cash needs us back in Heartwood Springs tonight."

"I'm going to use the bathroom and then I'll be right out."

———

I flush the toilet after using the bathroom, then wash my hands. I am eager to get going and see what awaits me in Sweetheart Bay. I hope it's a place I will be able to stay for a while, but I can't get used to that idea.

I look out the window before I go outside, and a calmness settles over me. Bryce, Brian, and John all are smiling. The three of them look so happy and I hope their good spirits continue. They have shown me such kindness and, despite the circumstances, I'm glad to be a part of the Reapers Wings.

I walk out the door and John looks up at me. "I guess this is goodbye."

John shakes his head. "That's where you are wrong, Andy. It's not goodbye. I have to see that you all make it out of here okay."

Baby starts whining and jumps up on me. The last thing I care about is getting dirt on my clothes. Baby smothers me with kisses when I bend down to pet him.

Bryce hands me my helmet and then cranks up his motorcycle. "Hop on and let's get going while the day is still young."

Brian is already on his motorcycle, ready to kiss this place goodbye. "You will be able to get freshened up when we get to Sweetheart Bay."

I hop on the back of Bryce's motorcycle and hold onto his waist. "Try not to go fast on this thing or I'll be sick."

Bryce laughs. "You better hold on tight and don't let go."

John gets in his car with Baby and slowly pulls out of his driveway.

I look around me everywhere, but don't see anyone or anything. The only thing I see is mountains upon mountains, which isn't such a bad thing. I may not have liked living in Heartwood Springs, but the mountains are one of my favorite things.

Bryce stays a safe distance away from John. "Not much longer until we are out of this county."

That makes me sad and gives me comfort at the same time. "I wish I could put my toes in the sand at the beach."

"You better get used to being cooped up in the house all day."

John's tires squeal as the car comes to an abrupt stop. He flings the door open, and Baby flies out, lips pulled back, teeth bared. Bryce brings the bike to a halt as Baby's barks echo through the early morning.

"Go get 'em, Baby! Kill 'em!" John yells.

I stare in horror when Baby jumps out of the car.

Bullets sail through the air, narrowly missing my head.

Bryce pushes me off of the motorcycle and my knees smack the gravel. Pain cuts deep as my skin drags across the coarse ground. "Get behind John's car and don't fucking move."

I crawl on the ground and make myself comfortable behind John's car. The bullets are no longer sailing pass me. They are heading in the opposite direction, towards Brian.

Brian exchanges gunfire back and says, "I tell you right now, you are a fucking dead man."

Bryce crawls over to where I'm sitting. "I didn't mean to push you so hard."

I shake my head. "It's okay."

"This will all be over soon. There's only one guy."

"How do you know?" I ask.

"We aren't getting gunfire from multiple directions," Bryce answers.

Baby makes his way up the hill with growls erupting from his lips. Seconds later, he goes behind a bush and clamps his teeth down on a man's arm. He has a death grip with no sign of letting up anytime soon.

The guy screams as Baby takes a big bite out of his arm. "Your fucking dog had to go and ruin everything."

Baby lets go of the man and John holds him back. Bryce and John both have their guns trained on the man so he won't do anything else.

John's face is beaming and he roars with laughter. "Good boy. That's the way to show him to not come creeping around on my property."

"Hugh promised me one hundred thousand dollars to bring Andy back to him," the man announces.

It makes me sick. "You don't mean shit to him. The only thing you are is his errand boy. Hugh's going to kill you because you aren't going to be doing what he asks."

"Why the fuck did you come out here all alone?" Bryce asks.

I am wondering the same thing.

"I was the only one close by who lives in this town," the man answers.

Brian looks at John. "We need to kill him so we don't have to worry about seeing his face around here again."

John takes a knife out of his pocket. "I have a much better idea for this fucker. Maybe it will teach him a lesson."

Beads of sweat run down the man's face. "Please don't. I had no idea what I was getting myself into."

"You should have thought things through before you came here," Brian answers.

The man tries to run away but Bryce grabs onto his shirt. "You're not going anywhere, so don't even think about it."

Growls erupt from Baby's lips and his teeth latch onto the man's leg. Panic washes over the man's face and his lips tremble. He looks like he's going to cry.

Bryce holds onto the man's arm and Brian grips onto his hand. John slices the man's pinky finger right off of his hand.

The man lets out a shrill scream. "What have you fucking done?"

Blood pours from his finger and nausea rolls through my stomach. A burning trail rises in my throat and I double over, puking all over the pavement.

John throws the finger at the man. "You're lucky I'm letting you off easy this time. You come back around here and I'll fucking kill you. You are a pathetic excuse for a human being, wanting to kill a sweet woman all because of money."

The color drains from the man's face. "I won't come back here again—" He stutters on his words before passing out.

Brian looks from the man to John. "Do you need us to stay here until he wakes up?"

John shakes his head. "I haven't made up my mind yet, but I think I might make things easy and just let Baby finish him off."

# ELEVEN

# PETE

RIDING my motorcycle does everything in the world to clear my mind of that bitch Natalie. The anger doesn't consume my soul anymore and I am at ease. I just hope the feeling lasts for the rest of the day.

There aren't many cars around. It's still early in the morning. Too early, if you ask me. It's only nine and things normally don't start getting busy until about ten. Then the parking lot becomes so crowded it's hard to get a parking spot.

Tommy pulls into the parking lot and I park my motorcycle beside his. "I need to know what you are thinking."

The two of us start walking towards the picnic tables. "My mind is clear right now, Tommy, and that's no bullshit."

He looks pleased with my answer. "Riding always helps give me a clear mind." He sits down at the picnic table and I join him. "I have been around a lot of people in my sixty years of living on this Earth, and you're the first person who has scared the shit out of me. The look you got on your face back there was something out of a horror movie."

"What can I say? I hate her fucking guts and want to kill her."

He shakes his head and then folds his arms across his chest. "Do you mind telling me what good killing her will do?"

"It will give me peace, knowing I won't have to be around her anymore."

"You've got to give me a better answer than that." He takes a cigarette out of his leather cut and lights it. "I remember when the two of you got together a hell of a long time ago. The two of you were just teenagers. You can't sit here and tell me you don't love her. It's nothing but bullshit you telling me that you hate her fucking guts. You wouldn't have been together with her all of those years if you didn't love her."

"Everything good I felt for her left me when I found her in bed with another man." I don't understand why we're talking about this right now. "She purposely let it happen yesterday to take a stab at my heart."

He blows out smoke, then takes another puff. "I can see your reasoning behind feeling upset, but not the hatred you feel for her. I've seen my fair share of jail time over the years and never once expected a woman to be waiting on me when I got out."

I don't like where he is going with this and my irritation grows. We may be from the same motorcycle club, but we didn't view things the same.

"All I know is I would have wrapped my hands around her neck and choked her to death. I'm pissed you wouldn't let me do that. It would have solved the problem of me being able to move on. She's the reason I was up early this morning, because I can't shake the image of her and that guy out of my mind."

"You can't shake that image out of your mind because you don't want to."

What he says is true. I haven't gotten over her yet. I just thought getting out of jail would mean getting back together with her. It was the one thing I had been looking forward to when I was locked up. I had held out hope our relationship could be restored.

"I guess you know me too well."

"I know when you love someone, you don't want to let them go." He puts out his cigarette and tosses the butt on the ground. "But, sometimes, the only thing we can do is try to make things work or move on with our lives."

"Things won't ever be able to work out between the two of us after everything that has happened." I think about Jaycee and how last night was amazing. I can't wait for us to fuck again tonight. It will help give me peace of mind so that I'm not consumed with rage. "I have another woman occupying my bed and that's what I look forward to."

"You've got the right idea when it comes to Jaycee, but not with Natalie." He diverts his gaze away from me to the black car that is pulling into the parking lot. "Killing Natalie won't help you move on. It will play on your mind and conscience like nothing has before."

I don't like how he thinks he knows how I will feel if I got the chance to kill her. He's not me and won't ever be me.

"I'll keep what you're saying in mind."

Hayden gets out of the black car and walks over to the two of us. "I didn't expect to see you two here this early, but I'm glad you're here. I can sneak you into the concession stand and give you some ice cream if you promise not to tell anybody."

Ice cream at nine in the morning sounds pretty good to me.

I stand up from the picnic table. "Anybody would be crazy to say no to ice cream. You can count me in."

Tommy rolls his eyes. "One ice cream and then we have to get back."

Hayden leads the way to the concession stand. "I promise that one ice cream isn't going to hurt you, Tommy."

"It isn't going to hurt me, but we have too much to do. We can't stay here all day," Tommy answers.

Hayden opens up the door to the concession stand. "I hope that it's not busy today. Nobody wants to work and most of my lifeguards are calling in. It makes me wish I hadn't agreed to run this place all summer long."

I make my way into the concession stand, enjoying the cool breeze from the air conditioner. "It sounds like an easy enough job, but I guess people just don't want to work."

"There is no guessing to it. People don't want to work," Tommy says.

I'm sure he knows, since he owns a strip club at Sweetheart Bay.

Hayden walks into the freezer and comes back out with two ice cream sandwiches. "I hope that these ice creams are alright. It's about the only thing I have left."

I take the ice cream sandwich out of the wrapper. "Hell, you're giving us free food. The last thing I'm going to do is complain."

"Just because you're not, I'm going to," Tommy says.

Hayden lets out a sigh. "I should have known you would have shit to say, Tommy."

Tommy shrugs. "I would have preferred a scoop of ice cream in a cup."

I take a bite of the ice cream sandwich, enjoying how

cold it is. "Are you still working at Reapers Wings Bar and Grill too?"

Hayden nods. "I'll probably never quit that place, unless Cash get rids of me. I like working there too much to leave. I'm just happy that Cash is okay with me running the pool during the summer."

Cash wouldn't get rid of her unless something horrible were to happen. She is someone we all trust and consider a friend.

Tommy takes a look around the room, probably looking for somewhere to sit down. "Cash isn't going to get rid of you, so you don't have to worry about that." He takes a bite of his ice cream sandwich. "He is going to need all the help he can get. Darcy will be out of work for the next couple of weeks."

I finish eating the rest of my ice cream sandwich. "I'm sure he'll hire more people before then to pick up some of the slack. I wouldn't worry too much about not being able to work a lot now, Hayden."

Hayden looks at Tommy like he's said something foreign. "What happened to Darcy? She was at the clubhouse yesterday, so I thought that everything was fine."

Tommy eats his ice cream sandwich before answering her. "She was beaten and left for dead last night."

Hayden looks shocked. Nothing like this has ever happened to a club member's old lady before. "Do they know who did it? I am going to have to go see her in the next couple of days. That makes my heart hurt. Poor Darcy didn't deserve that."

Tommy lies right through his teeth. "We have no idea who beat her."

I wonder why he's telling Hayden this. Maybe it is just to make small talk.

"I sure hope that you find him," Hayden says.

"I'm sure we will." Tommy turns to me. "I guess we better get going. Thanks for the ice cream and the chat."

I throw the wrapper in the trash. "Just keep the doors locked, Hayden. Call us if you need us."

Hayden doesn't look frightened or scared. She is known to have several guns, so she knows how to take care of herself. "Thank you for the heads up. I guess you can never be too careful."

"That's right. You can't be," Tommy replies.

Hayden turns on the television as Tommy and I are making our way outside.

"On our special newscast today, we have Hank Anderson on the FBI's wanted list. He's wanted for the brutal killing of Officer Jeremy Sanchez. This suspect is considered armed and dangerous. Proceed with caution if you encounter him and call the authorities immediately."

Hayden turns the channel on something else. "I would go crazy if I didn't have this television on, considering how quiet it would be in here."

Tommy acts like he's in a hurry all of a sudden. "I think that I would go crazy, too. See you later, Hayden."

Tommy's strides are quicker than mine and I pick up my speed.

"Would you mind telling me what's going on?" I ask.

Tommy stops walking when we are seconds away from reaching the motorcycles. "Hank is one of the ones involved with Darcy's assault. He's probably caught word of being on the FBI's wanted list by now."

Holy fucking shit.

Killing Hank was going to be pretty fucking hard now.

"I'm sure he's in hiding."

"There is no doubt in my mind we will still be able to find him and kill him."

The two of us continue walking to our motorcycles.

I have another question. "Why did you tell Hayden about Darcy?"

"No reason. I just know the two of them work together, so I thought why the hell not?"

# TWELVE

# CASH

THE WATER from the shower spraying on me feels amazing on my skin. I wish I could stay under longer, but I have too much to do today. I quickly wash up and rinse the shampoo out of my hair before getting out.

I grab a towel from the towel rack and wrap it around my waist before going back into the bedroom. Darcy is awake and her beautiful face is black and blue. "Do you need me to get you anything?"

Tears roll down her face and she shakes her head. "I just want to stay here in your arms all day, but I know you can't do that."

I go over to her and wrap my arms around her. The hardest thing I have ever done is not let my anger get the best of me. If I let my anger overcome every part of me, I would kill everyone in my path, no matter who the fuck they were.

"I'll tell you what. I will come back here in a couple of hours and bring you lunch." I hate it's the only thing I can do."I'm sorry, baby. I promise I won't be long when I come back to check in on you."

She pushes the tears away with her hand. "You're a busy man. I understand that. Just being around you makes things ten times better."

I know where she is coming from because being around her instantly makes my day so much better. There is no way to describe the peace and reassurance I always feel with her nearby. "I know, baby. Tonight I can promise you I will be here without leaving your side."

She gets up from the bed and turns her back to me. "I can't stay in bed feeling sorry for myself."

I don't like to hear those words come out of her mouth. "Darcy, you can stay in here all day if you choose to. You've experienced something horrible."

Her hands shake when she reaches for her panties in the drawer. "Fuck." She slams the drawer shut in frustration and anger. "I know you have a million things to do today, but I'm starving. Can you please fix me something to eat?"

There is a knock on the bedroom door and it doesn't surprise me to hear Nancy. I figured she would have come over here earlier asking questions. "Martin showed up at my house last night. I would like to know what's going."

"I'll be out there in a couple of minutes." I take off my towel and quickly dry myself. "Do you mind fixing us something to eat?" I ask, knowing the answer is going to be yes. "Darcy is absolutely starving."

"Alright, then. I will go see what I can find." Nancy sounds like she's eager to cook for us.

Darcy gets out a pair of panties and bra from the dresser, then puts them on. Her ribs are a mixture of purple and black. Today is going to be painful for her. It breaks my heart I won't be able to comfort her. "Nancy is good at saving the day."

"Darcy, I would have cooked for us."

She turns around so she's facing me. The pain on her face seeps down deep in my soul. "I know that you would have. I just don't want to stop you from doing what you need to do."

I press my lips against her forehead. "Sweetheart, you would not have been stopping me from doing anything."

She pulls away from me to walk over to the closet. Instead of putting on her clothes, she puts on my shirt instead. The shirt is long on her and comes right above her thighs. "I am going to talk to Nancy today. I think it will help."

It would be good for the two of them to talk about things. Even though they were already well acquainted with one another. I don't know. Maybe the thing that she needs to talk about is God. If that's the case, then Nancy is the person to talk to, because she believes God is the answer to everything.

I quickly slip into my usual black attire of black shirt, black underwear, and black socks. I also put on a pair of old jeans. "You should spend some time with her. She would enjoy your company."

She pulls on a pair of booty shorts before sitting on the bed. "Can you ask Nancy to bring me breakfast after she gets finished cooking?"

I walk back into the bathroom to put on my leather cut. "Don't worry about that, baby. I'll bring it to you myself."

"I'm not ready to face everyone yet."

I quickly brush out my shaggy blonde hair then brush my teeth. I desperately need a haircut, but Darcy likes my hair best like this and I promised to not cut it. "You take your time with that. We'll always be here."

She gives me several pecks on the lips, and I shut the bedroom door on my way out.

Slash is now sitting on the couch. "How is Darcy doing?"

"She's hanging in there."

Nancy has an egg sandwich ready for Darcy. "Do you want a sandwich, too, Slash?"

Slash nods. "I would appreciate it, Nancy. Thank you."

I take the egg sandwich in the bedroom to Darcy, who is holding onto her ribs. Seeing her in so much pain triggers the monster inside of me. My fists clench at my side. I imagine Hank and Liam's faces when I beat them to death. How bittersweet that is going to be. "Baby, here is your sandwich. Let me get you some ice for those ribs."

She takes the sandwich from me and begins devouring it. I wish she would have told me how hungry she was last night. I could have cooked her something then. "I hate to ask you, but can you get me a pack of veggie straws and another water too?"

I hurry back into the kitchen and get her everything she needs.

I see Pete and Tommy pulling into the driveway from the kitchen window. The two of them don't bother knocking on the door to my house. They just walk right in.

"Sorry we are late. I wanted Pete to get some anger out of his system." Tommy takes one look at me and I can tell he isn't happy. I wonder what could have possibly happened this morning. "Let's just say it has been an interesting morning."

Pete takes one look at Tommy, then back at me. "At least we saw what we did back at the marina."

Slash and I both exchange gazes with one another. "I'm going to take Darcy what she needs. I don't want to keep her waiting."

When I walk into the bedroom, Darcy has almost

finished eating her sandwich. "Thank you. I'm all set for the day."

I set her veggie chips and ice pack down beside her. "Me and the boys will be downstairs in the basement, talking. If you need anything, just call me. When I leave, Nancy and Martin will both be here with you."

"Do you think that today will be the day?"

She doesn't have to say the word *murder*. I know exactly what she is talking about.

"We are going to put everything in motion today." I hate not being able to give her a straight answer. "It could be weeks, or months even, but I hope it's sooner rather than later. You deserve to have peace knowing those scums will never walk the earth anymore."

She opens up the pack of veggie chips and takes a bite. "If you did things yesterday, would things have been different?"

"Things would probably be a lot different." We had given the three of them a head start. My guess was the three of them probably left town. They would have if they were smart, anyway. "But that doesn't matter. Last night you needed me."

She seems satisfied with that answer and doesn't say anything else. "Stay safe out there today. Try to stay out of trouble with the law."

A big grin appears on my face. This was something my Darcy would say. "You know me, sweetheart. I can't make any promises to that."

She gives me a goodbye kiss. "I love you."

"I love you too, baby, and don't you ever forget it."

———

Martin, Slash, Pete, and Tommy are all sitting at the table. Nancy has whipped them all up egg sandwiches and they are stuffing their faces. When she sees me, a frown appears on her face. It's been a long time since I've seen her this upset. "I can't believe that happened to Darcy. She's lucky she's not dead."

I don't know everything that Slash had told her. We are treading on murky waters because club business is club business, which means only members of the club know what is happening.

"I know I told her she needs to come out of her room today." Darcy being alone would be the worst thing for her. Everything would keep replaying in her mind over and over again. "Do you mind checking on her if she's not out in about an hour?"

Nancy knows I am not going to say anything else about Darcy. She knows better than to pry information out of me. "The two of us need to talk anyway. It's been a while."

Catch up would most definitely be good.

I turn to my brothers. "Let's go downstairs and talk."

Nancy hands me my plate of food before I leave the kitchen. "I'll be praying that you will make the right decision, Cash."

I don't say anything else to her. The last thing I want is to be angry or upset. The right decision in her eyes would be let God handle this situation and that's not going to happen. I have to kill each and every single one of them. I wouldn't be at peace if I didn't.

I lead the way down the stairs into the basement. As soon as I situate myself at the head of the table, I light a cigarette. Every single part of my body relaxes when I take that first puff. I feel more content and at ease. I always light a cigarette after waking up.

One by one, everyone sits down at the table before I dial Brian's number. He picks up on the first ring. "We all got here in one piece with Andy, and we are getting ready to head out."

Brian had called me about the shootout that happened last night.

"Are the two of you alone?" The two of them can't be here with us but still need to know what's going on.

Bryce starts talking. "We are now, and you're on speaker."

I let the words come pouring out. "I want you all to know just how much you mean to me. Last night every single one of you, in more ways than one, helped me keep my head on straight. If it wasn't for you all, I probably would've done something stupid."

Slash shakes his head. "No, you wouldn't have. You're smarter than that."

I have been around him my entire life, but I don't think he's right about that. I have never been consumed by so much rage. The hatred consumes me, and it's what fuels the blazing desire to kill. My heart shattered last night and the blaze burns from within. I want to see their lifeless bodies laying on the ground. It will make Darcy so proud.

I take several puffs of my cigarette. "I made a promise to Darcy that I would take care of what happened to her."

"That isn't something we need to vote on," Pete chimes in. "The answer should be a yes from every single one of us. We would want to do the same thing if it happened to our old lady."

"You already know I'm for it, brother." Slash rarely ever votes no in any matter. He never lets me down. "We just have to figure out exactly who we need to kill and when it will be possible."

"I hate to cut things short, Cash, but we have to get going." Brian sounds anxious and I know they have a long road ahead of them. "You do whatever you need to do so that Darcy can be at peace."

Bryce sounds excited when he speaks. "You already know that answer is a yes from me."

I take several puffs of my cigarette. "I will keep you all informed with everything that's going on."

---

Pete speaks with his mouth full. "What did Darcy say about the guy who beat her?"

"She didn't recognize him. She just said he had a swastika tattoo on his hand and his name is Liam." He has to be working for Hugh, but we need to find out who he is. "He's got to be a Southern Demons. It's the only thing that makes sense." The Southern Demons are known to have swastika tattoos and racist tattoos all over their body.

Pete has a crazy look in his eye. "He was the same guy who was fucking Natalie yesterday. He's got to be."

Martin looks surprised. "I know that Laken hasn't gone far. Hugh doesn't give a shit about her. He probably gave her drugs in exchange for helping him out. She just got out of rehab about a month ago."

I put out my cigarette and then slam my hand on the table in frustration. "I fucking want her dead by tomorrow."

Slash reaches across the table and squeezes my hand. "Easy now, brother. We have got to think this through."

I light another cigarette so I can keep calm. "We'll go by the restaurant first. I'll talk to Andrew. I'm sure he can point us in the right direction. He knows where everybody lives and everything that goes on."

Pete still has the same crazy expression on his face. "I want to be the one that kills Natalie when it's time."

I'm not going to mention that Natalie is part of the reason Darcy is still alive. I can't say that I trust her, but for now she is going to remain unharmed.

"We are already going to have enough blood on our hands, Pete," I say. "We don't need to think about killing anyone else besides Liam, Hank, or Laken."

For the first time, Tommy speaks up. "The two of us have already had this conversation, Pete. You don't want to kill her. You just think that you do. Cash, the two of us need to talk in private after we get done here."

If I had a guess this has something to do with Natalie. "We will do it, Tommy."

"Our chances of killing Hank are slim today." Tommy takes a good look at me. "He's on the FBI's most wanted list. I have to guess he's probably in hiding."

Tommy saying that infuriates me, since I was hoping I could kill him today. Right now, the focus was not going to be on killing Hank. The main focus would be on Laken and Liam. I have hope that at least one of them was close by.

"Liam was shot last night in the shoulder and could very well be in the hospital in town." I am almost positive that Liam wouldn't check himself into a hospital in this county. But it wouldn't hurt to find out. "I want both Tommy and Pete to go to the hospital and find out what you can. If he's not there, then we can search the hospitals nearby."

"Laken will be the easiest person to kill." Martin only states the obvious. "I don't think that she has anywhere to go. The girl doesn't even own a car and hasn't for years. I think she should be our primary focus today."

"I hope you're right about that, because I want her dead today." I will never forget Laken's hands on Darcy's neck, trying to choke the life out of her. I grit my teeth and the demons simmer to the surface. My hatred for Laken runs so deep I can snap her neck in a heartbeat. She is completely dead to me. "I'm telling you right now, things aren't going to be good if I don't have blood on my hands."

"Me and Tommy will go to the hospital and see what's up." Pete is the one who speaks up. "If Liam isn't there, I think we should just focus on finding Laken today. We will have an entire crew with us tomorrow. That will give us a chance to spread out better then."

I like where Pete's going with this. To me, it makes sense to just focus on one person, as bad as I hate to. The nearest hospital out of this county is an hour away. "That's settled then. The focus today is going to be on finding Laken. But I still want Pete and Tommy going to the hospital in town, just to be sure that Liam isn't there."

Slash nods. "Seems like a good idea to me, focusing on one at a time. I know you want all of them dead brother, but it makes things easier this way."

Tommy leans across the table and gives me a hug. "You'll get your revenge, Cash. I'm not leaving until the jobs get done."

Him saying that gives me comfort. He's the definition of a real brother and friend.

Tommy pats my shoulder before letting go of me. "Thank you for being here, Tommy. It means more to me than you will ever know."

Tommy nods. "I've always considered you the little brother I never had."

Slash points to my sandwich and looks at me. "I would eat if I was you. We have a big day ahead of us."

I put out my cigarette and grab my sandwich to go. "I do

believe that we are done here." I turn to Martin. "Do you mind staying here with Nancy and Darcy?"

Martin doesn't seem the least bit bothered by it. "Of course I can."

"Is anyone here opposed to me getting revenge for what happened to Darcy?" I ask.

Every single one of my brothers shake their head no, so this meeting is officially over. I just don't have my gavel with me because it is back at the clubhouse.

"I'll see everyone upstairs except for Tommy," I say.

The boys file out of the basement so that Tommy and I can be left alone. "Pete was dead set on killing Natalie today. She came by the clubhouse to get the car Andy left."

I am grateful for Tommy being here to keep him under control. "I don't want anything to happen to her, Tommy. She helped keep Darcy alive."

"I'll watch Pete while I'm here but when I'm gone, you need to keep your eye on him." He looks me straight in the eye. "It will only be just a matter of time before he kills her."

## THIRTEEN
## DARCY

I SEE Cash leave from the bedroom window. Tears form in my eyes because I just want him to stay here with me today, but I know that he's out there doing what he needs to do. So that I will be able to sleep at night.

I do want the three of them dead and I'm glad he's going to kill them. When it boils down to it, I don't think I'd ever be capable of killing someone. It's not something I'd be able to live with. At least I don't think so, but I've never even came close to doing such a thing.

I wipe the tears away with my hand and get out of bed. I'm not going to stay in here all day and feel sorry for myself. I am going to go talk to Nancy and Martin even though my entire body hurts. I don't need to be alone.

Martin is sitting on the couch when I walk out of the bedroom. As soon as he sees me, he gets up. "How are you doing?"

I let the tears roll down my face. "I'm not doing so hot, but I couldn't be alone."

He pats my back with his hand. "Cash should be back in a couple of hours."

I sit down on the couch and wince in pain. I wish I had some painkillers, something stronger than Tylenol, but I will be able to tough it out. "Where's Nancy?"

"She went downstairs to clean up after the boys."

That sounds like her. She always loves making sure that everything is super clean. "It couldn't be too dirty. I just cleaned up down there last week."

"It's not. Just a couple of plates is all."

"So when do you think you will buy a house?" I ask changing the subject.

It is time to play catch up, since Martin is Cash's cousin.

He rolls his eyes. "I don't need no damn house when I don't even have a woman."

You would think he'd like his own space and privacy, even though he loves the club more than anything. "I know if Cash didn't have this house, I might not have even got together with him."

What I say isn't entirely true, but at least it does sound good.

I love the clubhouse and the boys, since they are my family.

"I'm not really looking for a woman right now. I like having my freedom."

He just turned thirty, so I shouldn't be surprised with his answer. "The right woman will walk into your life when you're not even looking."

"The right woman has to be pretty damn good in bed for me to settle down with her."

"Sex isn't everything."

"Says the woman who Cash has sex with multiple times a week."

I don't know what to say to that because he is right. I wonder what Cash said to him about our sex life.

Nancy comes out of the basement with a stack of dishes in her hand. "I wish Cash would stop smoking."

"You can keep dreaming, Nancy. That's never going to happen," Martin replies.

Nancy takes a good look at me before going into the kitchen. "Darcy, would you want to go to church with me sometime?"

It is a question that Nancy has asked me many times before. My answer has always been no. I haven't set foot in a church in years, but going back might give me some peace. "Sure. Just let me know when."

Nancy's entire face lights up. "Oh, believe me, I definitely will."

Martin's cell phone rings and he leaves the living room to be alone.

"Do you think this is the reason this happened to me?" I have thought about it over and over again.

Nancy stops washing the dishes just for a second as she thinks about her reply. "I don't think so. I think it should be just a wakeup call for you."

Cash doesn't go to church, pray, or read the Bible. He doesn't think that God would forgive a sinner such as him. His reasoning is crazy because God forgives everyone. It doesn't matter who you are or the sins you have committed.

"I guess I do understand that. It's been a while since I've been to church and even prayed."

"Can you promise me something, Darcy?" Nancy asks.

"I don't know. It depends on what you want me to promise, Nancy."

"When you and Cash have children, I want you to make sure they go to church."

I couldn't imagine not letting our children go to church. Even if Cash would never go. I was going to make it a point to teach our children about God and being a Christian. I wouldn't imagine doing things any other way.

"That's a promise I can keep."

Martin walks back in the living room, interrupting our conversation. "It's a good thing I answered my phone, or Pam would have been on her way here."

Pam is Martin's mother and Nancy's sister. She lives in Sweetheart Bay and comes in more than she lives there. Martin is her only child and she calls him daily to check up on him. It annoys the crap out of him, so he occasionally won't answer his phone.

Nancy finishes up washing the few dishes, then sits down at the table. For the first time, I notice bags under her eyes. Martin staying with her last night must have been the reason for her restless night. "Well, that's Pam for you. She only worries herself sick like I do."

It got me thinking about my mother. I haven't talked to her much in the past couple of weeks and I feel bad about that. When I left Heartwood Springs five years ago, I left without telling her goodbye. My father's death had taken a toll on me and I had to get away in order to deal with my grief and pain. We haven't seen each other much in the past five years, but sometimes we talk to each other on the phone.

Martin run his hands through his shaggy brown hair. "She worries about me a little too much if you ask me."

"I'm jealous she lives at the beach." It has been two years since I have been on vacation and that is far too long. I long to put my feet in the ocean and lay on the beach without a worry in the world. "I wish, if Cash ever proposes to me, that would be where we could go on our honeymoon."

I want nothing more than to be Mrs. Daniels. It is

something I have wanted ever since the two of us got together. He is the biggest reason I wish I had come back sooner. I missed having someone to talk to every day. Being in Texas made me feel so alone and out of place.

Martin shuts his eyes and leans back against the couch. "I highly doubt the two of you are going to be going anywhere any time soon."

He is supposed to tell me what I want to hear, not kill my mood or give my hopes up. "I hope that you're wrong about that, because I need to get away from this place sometime this summer. Getting away will do us both some good so that we can be alone."

"Do you mind if I clean up your bedroom and bathroom?" Leave it to Nancy to want to clean all day.

I wasn't going to stop her from cleaning, because it was painful for me to even bend over. Me cleaning was out of the picture, at least for a little while until my ribs healed. "No, go right ahead. Thank you, Nancy."

Nancy gives me a warm hug. She is the sweetest woman I know and I can't wait for her to be my mother-in-law. "I'll come back by here in a couple of days to cook and clean and make sure you're doing okay."

"I sure do appreciate you, Nancy." The last thing on my mind is housework. It feels good to have that load lifted off my shoulders. "Thank you for making me that egg sandwich today. It was so good."

Nancy has always been soft spoken and is now. "You tell me what you would like me to cook and I'll go to the store, maybe later today."

I already have multiple things in mind. "I will definitely let you know."

Nancy has always been an amazing cook. Being in the kitchen has always been one of her favorite things. She makes the best chicken and dumplings and even makes homemade biscuits. No matter what she cooks, it is always delicious.

Martin opens up his eyes when Nancy goes in the bedroom. "We are all going to take care of things for you, Darcy. Don't go thinking we are not."

It makes me being down so much better. I don't have to worry about anything other than getting better. "I appreciate you staying here too, Martin. I know you want to be with the guys."

Martin shakes his head. "I want to be here, making sure that you and Nancy are safe. The two of you are family."

"Is Cash going to propose to me any time soon?" He can probably tell me the answer to that question since the two of them talk all of the time.

He keeps a straight face, so it's impossible to know if he's lying or not. "You're asking the wrong person. I'm not telling you shit. The two of us know that, even if he was, that's supposed to be a surprise."

Not knowing if he has been planning on proposing or not was absolutely killing me. I never did find an engagement ring anywhere, and I had looked through nearly everything. He was either good at hiding it, or hadn't got me one at all.

"You saying that is not helping anything."

He laughs. "It helps everything concerning me just fine."

A convertible pulls into the driveway. I glance out the window because I don't recognize the vehicle from anywhere. What if one of them had come here to finish me off? My heart beats fast and I think about Martin and Nancy. They would surely kill the two of them too.

Martin puts his arm around me. "I'm going to take care of whoever this is. You just need to calm down."

Martin's mother gets out of the convertible. I wonder what Pam is doing here, considering Martin had just talked to her minutes ago.

"I guess your mother decided to pay you a visit."

He folds his arms across his chest and grumbles. "I don't know why. It's not like I haven't seen her in forever. She just came in last month and stayed for a week. That week was the longest week of my life."

Pam starts to knock on the door, but Martin lets her in before she can. "I figured you would be here with Nancy and Darcy. Tommy let me know what is going on. I was bored, so I decided to come see you."

"Everything is just fine, Pam." Martin comes back over to the couch and sits down. "It's not anything we won't be able to handle."

Pam steps inside and shuts the door behind her. "Are you telling me I'm not allowed to worry about you? Is that it?"

He lets out a sigh in defeat. This isn't an argument he is going to win. "Can you just tell me how long that you're staying?"

Pam ignores his question and sits down beside me. "They sure did a number on you, that's for sure."

That was putting things kindly. It's no secret that Pam doesn't hold anything back. "I couldn't do anything because they threatened to kill Berkley. She was there with me."

"I would have done whatever I could to get away from them." Her words are harsh and that's where the two of us aren't the same. I couldn't live with Berkley's life being lost because of me. Besides, there was no way I could have escaped out of that room. "Chances are they were probably all talk and we're never going to do anything to her to begin with."

I have never looked at things that way, but I have a feeling she is wrong about that. "Even if that's the case, I don't regret not fighting back."

She grins at me real big. "I guess that you're a better person than me, because I wouldn't have given a damn what happened to my friend. I would have made sure I came out of there without any harm done to me. But then again, I can't say I even have many friends. I guess that's the reason why."

FOURTEEN
# CASH

ANDREW'S black truck is the only vehicle when I arrive at the bar. He's not going to be happy with me, considering Darcy is supposed to work today. I haven't made arrangements to call in anyone else either, so he will probably have to work her shift himself.

I find Andrew in the back with his head in his hands. When he sees me, he raises up his head to look at me. "Where's Darcy? It would have been nice to get a phone call saying she can't work today."

I tell it to him like it is. "I'm sorry, but Darcy was beaten up last night."

His eyes widen and he stares at me in disbelief. "Damn. What can I do?"

"Tell me where Laken Head would go if she was trying to hide from the club."

Sometimes he acts like it bothers him when I ask him about people. He still allows his conscience to get the best of him after all these years. It's something I still don't quite understand. "Please don't tell me she's behind this."

Technically, she isn't the only one behind this. But he

doesn't need to know that because it isn't any of his business. He doesn't need to know every person involved or everything that is going on.

"I'm afraid so, or I wouldn't give a shit about where we could find her."

"She is probably at Donald McKenzie's house, but I don't know for certain."

Donald McKenzie works at Heartwood Springs Hospital as a custodian. The last time I was at the hospital several months ago, he was working in the afternoon. I have to make sure that hasn't changed.

The best part about where he lives is there aren't any houses for miles, so no one would know anything. It will be easy to get in and get out. I can't think of a better scenario.

"Let's hope you're right about that, for both of our sakes."

"Laken is trying to get her life together. Her and Donald just got engaged not long ago."

I don't want to hear him talk about my victim. My mind was made up last night when Laken had her hands wrapped around Darcy's neck. She is lucky I hadn't killed her right then, because I would have if it hadn't been for Darcy.

I don't feel anything anymore if I commit a murder. I don't let it weigh on my conscience because it's not personal to me. I don't give a shit about the people I kill. Every single one of them deserves to die.

"Laken must not be trying to get her life together, since she's hanging around drug dealers."

He shakes his head. "I don't think you're right about that. She just got out of rehab."

Why does he actually believe that she has changed? The girl has been to rehab three times in the last two years. If she wanted to change, she would have by now. "Andrew, would you listen to yourself talk? It's the biggest load of bullshit I've ever fucking heard."

"You don't even know her. Don't you have any faith? You know that people are capable of changing."

"So it's right that she played a part in Darcy getting beaten?" My temper is rising with each passing minute. This isn't a conversation that needs to happen. "The most precious thing in my life will forever be scarred because of what happened. I don't give a fuck if she's changed or not. She is nothing but a junkie who deserves everything that is going to happen to her."

"What are we going to do about Darcy? Because I take it she won't be here for a while."

We are going to have to do the thing we should have done a long time ago. "We're just going to have to hire someone else."

I have brought it up to Andrew over and over again about hiring other people, but he always dismisses me. He doesn't want to pay out the money when it comes to hiring someone else. Instead, he gets Darcy and Jaycee to work their asses off.

"I guess I will start doing interviews this week."

"Tell me when you're doing the interviews and I'll try to be here."

"What if Laken isn't where we think she is? Will you still be here then?"

I don't know why he asked that question, because he already knows the answer to it. "I don't know. I can try to be, but I'm not promising anything."

"I hope you can be, because I need you."

"I know you do. If I can't work, I'll get Jaycee to cover my shift."

"You're the one I need here, not someone else."

Nobody is as quick on the grill as I am. They can't multitask like me. It is the biggest reason he had hired me to begin with. I have been working with food ever, since I was a teenager, so if I wasn't quick, something has to be wrong. It isn't my favorite thing in the world to do but I have to do something to pay the bills.

"I'll be here Monday through Friday. That is, if we can find Laken."

I would be spending every waking moment trying to find Laken, Hank, and Liam. I won't be able to get any rest until they are no longer walking on this earth.

He shakes his head, but doesn't press the issue farther. "I am hoping you can do me a favor and work for me Monday. I've got to go to the doctor and don't want to miss my appointment."

"If I can't be here, I will get someone else to be."

I was going to try to keep my word, though I wasn't sure I could.

He doesn't look convinced. "I hope you will be, because I have to have an MRI and don't want to reschedule."

I don't need or want to hear anymore. The two of us work well together, but we aren't friends. We will never be friends, because I won't allow it. "I'm going to get going. Thank you for the information."

He scratches his head. "I guess you're not going to ask me what's wrong."

I tell him nothing but the cold-hearted truth. "I can't get close to a person who could potentially end up being my enemy."

He laughs uneasily. "Why would you begin to think that?"

"You're a good guy, Andrew." He's like ordinary people, and I fear one day he would cross me. He is an informant, but has empathy and remorse, two things I try not to let weigh on my conscience anymore. "And I'm nothing but a cold-hearted fucking bastard."

He still looks uneasy as I leave the room. "I'll see you Monday, Cash."

"You can count on it."

I sure do hope that he could.

Slash is waiting for me outside. "I take it that you found the answers you were searching for."

Was the happiness on my face that obvious? "Let's head on out to Donald McKenzie's house."

He starts up his motorcycle and gets ready to ride. "I hope Andrew is right about this."

I sure as hell hope he is too, because if he's not, we are back to square one.

# FIFTEEN
## PETE

I HESITATE before I step into the hospital. Beads of sweat stream down my face and I crinkle my nose. I hate being here, since it reminds me of my father. He died in a hospital when I was a little boy. It's the reason I stay away from hospitals at all costs and Cash knows that, so he really owes me one.

Tommy goes up to the desk and I notice the woman's eyes are puffy. "We're wondering if you have a man named Liam here."

The woman doesn't even bother to look up his name in the computer. "Honey, I've been working ever since last night. I can promise you that nobody by the name of Liam has checked themselves in."

I take out my cell phone and pull up a picture of Liam from social media. "His name might not be Liam. It could be something else. Do you mind looking at a picture of him, just to be sure?"

The woman holds out her hand and then studies the picture for a couple of seconds. "I haven't seen the guy. I'm sorry, he's not here."

It wasn't like we would expect him to be here. He isn't stupid.

"Pete, is that you?" Shit, it is my grandmother. She's the woman who raised me and I haven't talked to her in months.

I turn around and glance at her. She looks so happy to see me that it wouldn't be right for me not to talk to her. After all this hospital is the hospital that she oversees. "Yes, Grandma, it's me alright. I just got out of jail yesterday. I was going to stop by your house today so I could see how you were doing."

Tommy mouths me the words. "What the fuck are you doing? We need to get going."

"She will be able to get us into rooms. She's the hospital administrator," I hiss.

Edith doesn't seem to hear Tommy and I talking to one another. She just turned sixty-five last month, so her hearing is going with her age.

She puts her hands on the side of my face to get a closer look at me. Old age has not only made her have hearing loss, but has also made her blind as a bat. "I can't believe that it's really you. I was so afraid you were going to forget about me."

"I could never forget about you, Edith. Now that's crazy talk." Maybe she would help us scour this hospital, looking for Liam. Chances are he's probably not here, but we have to make sure. "We are looking for somebody who got shot last night and could be here. I was wondering if maybe you could help us find him."

Edith nods. "I will help the two of you any way I can. This week is my last week working here anyway. It's about time I retired."

Tommy looks annoyed, but there's nothing I can do about it. I am just glad we can see for ourselves if Liam is here. The woman at the front desk might not know what the hell she's talking about.

Tommy speaks to Edith as politely as he can. "No disrespect to you, ma'am, but we can't be here all day at the hospital."

Edith stops walking to glance at Tommy. "You're telling me something I already know. Nancy called me this morning and told me about Darcy. I suppose that you're here looking for who did this to her."

My grandmother has been around the club long enough to make sense of what goes on.

"Yes, we are, but I don't think that he's here," Tommy answers.

Edith picks up her pace and uses her badge to open up the doors so we can look into the patient's rooms. "We've only got twenty patients here right now, so you should be able to see who you're looking for."

Tommy and I both peek in the rooms that we pass by, but see no Liam. It's discouraging, facing the reality that he's probably not here. Whenever Tommy's guys come down from Sweetheart Bay, we will be able to check out all of the other hospitals close by. Right now, the thing that we need to do is get back and regroup. We need to see what Cash wants to do next.

"Is there anyone in ICU?" I ask.

Edith shakes her head. "Not a single soul or I would take you down that way. The only person we had in ICU died last week, but I suspect we will be getting people soon. Several of the hospitals close by are getting ready to send some patients our way."

I give Edith a hug before parting ways. "Thank you for showing us around."

"Come by tomorrow and I'll feed you some supper," Edith calls after me.

I don't get a chance to reply back at the speed that Tommy and I are walking.

Tommy lets outs a sigh. "Damn, we didn't find nothing of importance here."

I look up and see Donald in the cafeteria, eating. "I think that we found our reason for being here."

Donald's eyes meet mine and he takes off running.

I am close behind him and nearly crash into people in my quest to get to him.

Tommy lags behind me. "Keep going! I'll catch up with you in a minute."

I follow Donald out the door and am stopped by the guy who was at the party last night.

Donald gets in his truck and disappears out of sight.

The guy has a smirk on his face. "I told you I would be seeing you around town."

I want nothing more than to punch his lights out. It takes every part of me to hold myself back. This guy probably knows I just got out of jail yesterday. It's no secret. He could very well want to pick a fight with me on purpose, just so that my ass would land back in jail. "Do you mind fucking telling me why you are here?"

The guy pokes my leather cut, trying to get a reaction out of me. "So that I can kick your ass."

I stare at him, wondering why he's acting like such a tough guy. "I'm not a swinger, man. Never will be. I don't have threesomes, or any of that shit, because I think it's crazy. Will it make you feel better, punching me in the face?"

"You're damn right it will, but it's not the reason I followed you out here."

"That's just too fucking bad, because you're the one who started this shit last night. You should not have touched Jaycee and just kept your hands to yourself. Let's end it right here and right now."

The guy puts a gun to my head. "The only way to end this is if you're dead."

I hold out my hands and begin to wonder what this crazy fucker is going to do next. "Payback doesn't mean killing me, man. All I did was punch you last night. That's it. You have no reason to have a gun pressed to my head."

Tommy is out of breath when he reaches the two of us. "Where the fuck is Donald?" He takes one look at the fucker from last night and the gun pressed to my head. "Put the gun down. It's not going to solve shit."

The guy shakes his head. "That's where you are wrong. It will solve a lot of things if I blow Pete's head off. Then maybe you will start talking and tell me where Andy is, because we know that she's heading to Sweetheart Bay."

It doesn't sit well with me, knowing this fucker was at the party last night, considering he's with the Southern Demons. We were going to have to be more careful with who we invite to our parties.

Tommy takes out his gun and presses it against the guy's back. "We aren't telling you shit about Andy, or anything concerning this club. If you want to blow Pete's brains out, you go right ahead, but know that you're going down next."

What Tommy says doesn't faze the guy. He's still holding strong. "You are playing with fire here when it comes to Pete's life. I can tell you right now I'm not afraid to die."

"I take it that you're Hugh's errand boy," I say. "He doesn't give two shits about you because you're easily replaced."

The guy smirks but doesn't let up on the gun. "You don't know shit about me, so I suggest you shut your fucking mouth."

"What I do know is that this is pretty fucking stupid," Tommy whispers in his ear. "We are in a public place. It's not going to take long for the cops to come rolling out here. Do you want to spend some time locked up behind bars for this? Not many of those boys behind bars are too fond of those Southern Demons. I have connections with the inside. Things aren't going to look good concerning you."

The guy lets go of me and lowers his gun. "It doesn't matter whether you tell me where Andy is or not, because she's going to be found. Hugh has over a dozen people looking for that bitch."

Tommy hits the guy in the back with the gun. "You're lucky I didn't beat the shit out of you. If you don't keep talking, I will."

The guy shrugs. "I just tell the Southern Demons what they want to know about all of you. It's been easy coming in your clubhouse the last couple of months unannounced."

Tommy puts his finger on the trigger. "What have you fucking told them about us?"

"The Southern Demons know everyone that you all associate with. What happened to Darcy is just the beginning. They want control over this county so they can bring drugs in from the cartel. I heard them say a thing or two about trafficking guns through here also," the guy tells us.

This guy is a pussy for giving in and telling us what we need to know. Going to prison must be weighing heavy on his mind. Tommy wasn't lying when he said that he has connections in the inside. Two of his buddies that I know of are in prison for murder. They have life sentences. They have nothing to lose when it comes to killing another inmate behind bars.

"When are they going to be moving in?" I ask.

"By the end of the week," the guy answers.

Tommy has a pissed-off look on his face. "Why the fuck are you telling us this?"

"Because I have had my eye on Jaycee for the past couple of months." His life is now over because he's a rat. He told us what the Southern Demons' plans are. "I don't want anything to happen to her."

I want to sock him a good one in the face, but I withhold myself. "Why did you stop me from letting Donald leave?"

"Because the girls are coming today," the guy says.

Tommy and I look at each other confused. "What girls are you talking about?" Tommy and I both ask at the same time.

An old beat-up car pulls into the parking lot and the guy takes off running. I chase after him, but don't get to him soon enough. I watch the car leave, still wondering what the hell the guy was talking about.

Tommy takes his phone out of his pocket. "I'm calling Cash to warn him not to go into Donald's house."

Several seconds pass by, with me waiting impatiently to see if Cash picks up.

Tommy hangs up the phone and starts dialing again. "You would think that of all times he would pick up his phone right now."

I just hope that Tommy will be able to reach him in time.

# SIXTEEN

# CASH

SLASH and I park our motorcycles at the bottom of an old dirt road leading into the woods surrounding Donald's house. It isn't a road that many people travel, so we would be coming to his house unannounced. The only crappy thing about it is we have to tramp through the woods to get a clear view of Donald's house.

The grass clearly hasn't been touched in months. The one thing I worry about is stepping on a venomous snake. I wouldn't be worried about stepping on a snake so much if I was wearing my boots, but I have put on my tennis shoes instead. The soles on the bottom of my boots are so worn down that I had to throw them away. I have had them for years and need to buy a new pair.

Slash seems as thrilled as I am to be tromping through the grass and overgrown brush. "You would think that he would take care of this shit instead of letting it look like this."

"He probably doesn't come out here much, if I had to guess."

"I don't see why. It would give him a bigger backyard."

I pat him on the shoulder. "If only other people thought like you and me."

Slash is the first one to get a clear view of Donald's house. "We aren't going down there and getting in his house today. There are far too many vehicles around."

Son of a fucking bitch, there are five vehicles parked in the driveway. The thing that is puzzling to me is none of those vehicles belong to Donald. He drives an old red truck and these vehicles are all brand new models. What the fuck is going on here?

I watch the house like a hawk for several seconds and a van pulls into the driveway. Asher steps out of the driver's side. He is a Southern Demons and was here ten years ago when he was just a teenager.

Slash shakes his head. "I don't have a good feeling about this."

"I just can't believe that we have let this happen."

Asher lets a girl out of the van. "You try anything, I'm going to spread those legs open and have my way with you."

The girl doesn't look much older than seventeen. "Why am I here?"

Asher slaps her across the face. "I didn't say for you to speak, now did I?"

I clench my fists and bare my teeth. I won't ever and will never tolerate women being a victim of rape. The girl is clearly here against her will. I am going to make sure that I find out everything.

I can't see straight when I begin walking towards the house. Slash grips onto my shirt, keeping me from taking another step.

"Let's think this through, Cash. You're as angry as I am. We can't go in there right now, brother. Think about how many people could be inside that house. It's a situation we don't want to get ourselves into yet."

I take a deep breath and try to get my anger under control. "Regardless of what happens with Laken, we are taken this place down tonight."

The girl begins to cry. "I just want to go back home and be with my family."

Asher grabs her by the arm. "Your home is with the Southern Demons now, so you better get used to it."

Slash nods. "That's what we need to do before things get out of hand. For now, we need to get back to the clubhouse and regroup."

It makes me wonder what Tommy and Pete found out at the hospital.

"I wonder what this place is. Do you think that it's a human trafficking ring or prostitution ring?"

Slash starts walking back towards the motorcycles. "The way that Asher was handling that girl makes me believe that it's one of the two."

"I wonder just how many girls have been brought here undetected."

Slash's eyes go dark. "Just one is way too many."

The minute we reach our motorcycles is when I see Donald's truck. He gets out of the truck with a gun in his hand. "I don't appreciate you boys coming up here and snooping around."

I stare coldly into his eyes. "I don't appreciate you involving yourself in kidnapping young girls and holing them up in your house."

Donald chuckles. "You don't have any fucking idea the shit that I do."

Slash stalks towards Donald and points his gun at him. "I would suggest you start talking about the shit you do that the Reapers Wings don't know about. We are the ones who control what happens in this county, not you or anyone else."

I see what appears to be a guy in the passenger's seat of Donald's truck. His gun is trained on Slash. "Slash, get the fuck down."

Slash puts his finger on the trigger and the two of us are sprayed in bullets. One of the bullets grazes his shoulder and he yells out in pain. "When I get ahold of you, I'm going to take my sweet time killing you!"

I fire my gun at the windshield and glass shatters everywhere. "We can end this right now if you just tell me where Laken is."

Donald fires his gun back, narrowly missing me. The bullet bounces off of a tree. "I broke up with that junkie last night, so I wouldn't know where the hell she is."

Slash makes himself comfortable out of harm's way behind an overgrown bush. "Holy fucking hell, getting shot wasn't what I had planned for today."

I step out from behind a tree to see where Donald is. His gaze is dead set on me and he fires his gun. The bullet hits the tree above my forehead. "You aren't going to win here, Donald, so I don't see why we are doing this."

Donald strolls towards me. "I am doing this because I hate your fucking guts, Cash. I have never liked you or this fucking club for sending my nephew Harry to prison. He just wanted to have a little fun with that girl and you should've let him."

Two years ago, at thirty, his nephew had been having sex with a girl who was only thirteen. A fucking child. We made sure his ass got sent to prison where he belongs.

It had taken every ounce of strength not to put a bullet in Harry's head. But we made a promise to the girl's mother and father that we wouldn't do him any harm. Their definition of justice is him being behind bars where he belongs.

Slash takes a peek at Donald from the corner of his eye. "Do you know who the fucker is in the truck?"

"I have no idea, other than someone afraid to play with the big boys," I reply.

Whoever is in the truck was a real pussy. I was certain that they weren't dead, even though they could have been hit when the windshield glass shattered.

Slash laughs through his pain. "We need to surprise Donald at the same time. He won't ever see us coming."

Donald fires his gun a little too close for my comfort, hitting the ground beside my foot. "You going to hide all day behind that tree, Cash?"

Slash signals for me to go and he shoots Donald in the arm, catching him off guard. Donald's gun falls to the ground. "Serves you right for grazing my shoulder with a bullet and believing that raping women is okay to do. You fucking, perverted, no good piece of shit."

I shoot Donald in the foot and he falls to the ground. "No, I'm not going to be hiding behind a tree all day, you stupid fuck. I know how to be smart with shootouts, which is something you need work on."

Slash gets the gun from the ground and presses it to Donald's head. "Tell us what you are doing with those girls."

Donald scowls. "Why the hell would I tell you anything, considering you're just going to kill me anyway."

I shove my finger in the bullet wound on his arm and it starts pouring blood. He screams and I couldn't be more pleased that I got my point across. "We aren't going to kill you, Donald. What we are going to do is make you bleed out." I turn to Slash, who still has the gun trained on Donald's head. "Go ahead. Shoot his other foot so he won't be able to walk out of here."

Slash shoots Donald's other foot. "Next, it's going to be the other arm, so I would suggest you start talking."

Donald holds out his hands. "Alright! Okay! We bring those girls so that people can bid on them. They buy the girls from us at an auction so they can be their sex slaves. I swear to you I'm not lying."

Slash spits in Donald's face. "You're a sick fuck who deserves to get everything that is coming to you."

I tug on Slash's shirt. "Let's go before we get bombarded by Southern Demons."

The two of us start walking, but Slash stops when we get to the truck. There is not an adult but a kid who is laying on the floorboard, in fear for his life. "We aren't going to hurt you, little fellow," Slash says.

The kid begins to cry, and nothing but anger consumes my soul. Why the fuck would Donald put this kid in harm's way? "Please tell me that my grandpa is going to be alright."

"Your grandpa Donald is going to be just fine," I answer.

Slash gives the kid a hug before letting him down. "Go in the house and tell them that your grandfather has been shot."

Tears are still pouring down the kid's face when he kicks me in the knee and says, "That's what you get for hurting my grandpa."

My knee throbs at the force behind that kick. "I would suggest you get going before I finish killing him."

The kid sticks his tongue out at me before he starts running. "Grandpa, I will be right back!"

I wobble my way back to my motorcycle, put on my

helmet, and start the engine. "Let's get going before those fuckers come out here and find us."

Slash cranks up his motorcycle. "You don't have to tell me twice."

———

Pete and Tommy are waiting on us down at the lake.

I pull into a parking space and Slash parks beside me. "We didn't find Laken down at Donald's house, but found a human trafficking ring instead."

Tommy's face is redder than a beet. "Do you not know how to pick up your phone when someone is calling you? I have called you about twenty times in the last thirty minutes. You fucking asshole."

I get my cell phone out of my pocket and realize it's on vibrate. I must have been so busy riding and dealing with Donald, I hadn't heard it. "I'm not the one that you should be worried sick about. That's Slash."

Slash pulls off his leather cut, then takes off his shirt. The scars will always be on his chest where he was stabbed multiple times fifteen years ago. That's how he had gotten his nickname.

The bullet wound doesn't look horrible. He's going to make it. The wound isn't deep enough to require a hospital stay. It can easily be stitched up when we get back to the clubhouse. He's just going to have to watch it to make sure it doesn't get infected.

Pete examines the wound and he looks intrigued. "How the fuck did that happen?"

"Donald McKenzie and his stupid ass." Slash starts to go off. "He started shooting at us with his grandson in the passenger seat. His grandson is just a fucking kid, probably no more than ten."

Tommy appears to be calmer and at ease. "I take it that the kid is okay."

"The kid is perfectly fine," I say.

I am glad that he is. I would never be able to live with myself if he wasn't.

# SEVENTEEN
# ANDY

THE SUN BLAZES down on my skin when we cross the bridge to go into Sweetheart Bay. I can't wait to get to wherever I am going so that I can take a shower. The sweat is seeping through my shirt. It's got to be at least ninety degrees out.

"We are almost there, Andy. You've just got to hang in there a little while longer." Bryce stops the motorcycle at a red light. "Then you will be able to eat and take a shower if you need to."

That gives me comfort, because I feel like there is a target on my back. I will be glad to not be out in the open. I glance over my shoulder at the vehicles around me, suspicion growing deeper, and the fear sets in. Any one of them could be a Southern Demons.

My eyes stop on the motorcycles straight ahead and I grip Bryce tighter. "I am guessing you want me to try to relax."

Brian looks at his watch on his wrist. "Yes, you need to relax, Andy. A couple of Tommy's guys are heading our way."

The question is will they get here soon enough?

The light turns green and Bryce moves forward. "Andy, you need to take out my gun and let them know we are coming."

I take out the gun from his pants with my hand shaking. "I can't say I have ever shot a gun before."

"I don't give two shits about that," Bryce answers.

I shoot at the Southern Demons like Bryce wants me to do. It catches them off guard and people on the street duck. Bryce speeds up and we begin exchanging the gun fire. "They're coming. Holy shit, they are fucking coming."

From a distance, it had looked like there was only a handful of them. But there are ten, possibly more. Chills run up and down my spine. It's me they are after. No one else. I just don't understand how they could know, out of all the places that I could be, to come here. I guess it has something to do with the Reapers Wings in Heartwood Springs being closest with the chapter here.

Brian rides alongside Bryce. "All we have to do is make it another quarter of a mile and then we'll be able to have some relief. Andy, we've gotten you this far. I promise you it will be over my dead body before someone takes you."

A lump forms in my throat. "I hope things won't come to that."

Bryce looks through his mirror and a scowl appears on his face. "They are coming up on us quick, so this is enough chitchatting. Andy, you better be ready to fire that gun again, because you're going to have to."

I don't have a chance to respond as Bryce speeds up and weaves in between two cars. Cars are on opposite sides of us, and the closeness makes me uncomfortable. All it would take is one wrong move for us to get hurt.

Brian is right behind us, acting as a shield for me. No

Southern Demons are going to get to me without going through him first. Not even my own family would do the things these men are doing for me.

I look over at the woman driving in the car alongside us. There is no doubt in my mind that she witnessed me shooting that gun, because she looks absolutely terrified. I wish I could see what I look like right now. I'm sure that my face matches her own.

I see the lights up ahead and Bryce speeds up to get past them. My heart flutters fast when the light turns yellow. I put his gun back in the holster, then hold onto his waist with both hands and squeeze tight. The lights turn red and I close my eyes as a car lays on the horn, then open them up again because the two of us are still alive.

The Reapers Wings are waiting for us at the Reapers Wings Dance Club. They are sitting on their motorcycles with their guns drawn. I nestle my head into Bryce's shirt and brace myself for the gunfire.

The bullets ring through the air when we pass by and Bryce keeps driving. I glance behind me quickly and see a Southern Demons getting ready to fire his gun at me. Brian is two steps ahead and takes him out with one shot. His motorcycle comes crashing down on the road and he flies through the air before landing back down.

A wave of relief washes over me. No more Southern Demons are trailing after us. For the first time since setting foot in Sweetheart Bay, I feel like I'm going to make it to the house in one piece.

———

My stomach twists in knots and nausea sets in when Bryce pulls into a beach house on the outskirts of town. "I think I'm going to be sick."

Bryce laughs. "Sick? Andy, come on now. That was fun. We are alive and breathing, the two things that make it so much better."

I take deep breaths and remind myself everything is going to be okay. "You are crazy. That was far from fun. My definition of fun is staying at home and watching movies all day. Not the shit that happened back there."

Bryce chuckles. "I guess watching movies at home all day is alright too."

Brian pulls into the driveway and takes off his helmet. "Let's go inside and see if there's some cold water in the fridge."

I walk into a house that is cool inside and sit down on the couch. "You said that this is Trevor's house?"

Could it possibly be the Trevor I had graduated high school with?

Bryce gets a water out of the fridge. "Yep, it's Trevor's house. He mentioned that the two of you went to high school together."

My cheeks turn red, thinking about the man who was once my Trevor. I can't believe that he is a Reapers Wings. It's been forever and a day since I have seen him or even spoken to him.

Thank God for him coming here and me not being with someone that I don't know. I take off my sneakers. "My day has just gotten ten times better."

Brian nearly drinks the entire bottle of water he has in his hands. "I wish Trevor would hurry up. We've got to get back on the road."

Bryce makes his way to the bathroom. "I'll be right back."

Trevor pulls into the driveway and walks up to the door with a bag in his hand. He hasn't changed a bit since I've seen him. He looks sexier now than he did so many years ago. His muscles are bulging underneath that leather cut and I've never known him to be so fit. "Andy, I'm glad to see that you're in one piece."

I give him a hug. "These guys helped keep me safe."

Brian pats Trevor on the shoulder. "We are going to get going after Bryce gets out of the bathroom. Call us if you need anything and we will come running."

Trevor nods. "You two have a safe trip going back. I'll be talking to you soon."

Brian stops at the door and looks at me. "I'll be seeing you, Andy. You're in good hands with Trevor here."

A wave of sadness washes over me. "Oh, I know. I'm in great hands."

Bryce gives me a hug before leaving. "Be good, Andy, and stay safe."

I try my hardest not to cry. "I hope our paths cross again, Bryce, but if they don't, just know I will never forget you."

Bryce leans down and kisses my cheek. "You know as well as I do that our paths are going to cross again. It was nice meeting you, Andy, despite the circumstances."

I watch the two of them leave from the window, and Trevor puts a comforting arm around me. "I hate that I had to say goodbye to them."

Trevor stares into my eyes. His green eyes are dreamy and enough to make any girl melt. "I hate that you did too, but they had to get back. Cash needs them at Heartwood Springs because a lot of shit is going down."

The shit that he is talking about has everything in the

world to do with Darcy. That much I do know. I hope Cash is able to get his revenge. "I never imagined in a million years you would be the one protecting me."

He leans back against the couch and I make myself comfortable in his arms. This is the perfect ending to a horrible day. "I'm glad that it's me and no one else, because we have a lot of catching up to do."

I wish I could get used to this, but the reality is I'll probably have to go somewhere else soon. This city is filled with Southern Demons. Many of them probably survived the shootout back there. "How long have you been a member of the Reapers Wings?"

"Two years. I'm a nomad." He leans down and kisses my forehead. "I don't belong to any specific chapter. I just go wherever they need me to be. I've been here in Sweetheart Bay for the past couple of months to give Tommy a hand. A couple of his guys are in jail and he needed the help."

That makes perfect sense, but the thing that doesn't make sense is this house. The house is nice, especially since it's ocean front. I was sure that it cost at least six figures or more. "How the hell can you afford this house?"

He chuckles. "I've been stripping ever since I turned twenty-one."

I can see women going crazy over him now. He may be thirty-six, but he's still sexier than ever with his muscular build and freshly-cut brown hair. I wish I had known about him being a stripper. I would have gone to one of his shows. "I guess that's one way of making an ass ton of money."

"I'm not going to lie, I enjoy the attention."

I shove him and he starts to laugh. "I should have known you were going to say something like that."

He changes the subject, not wanting to talk about it

anymore. "Tell me about how you wound up involved in all of this mess."

"I married a guy who turned out to be a psycho."

"Well, shit, that sounds like a hell of a story."

It is a hell of a story, and one I don't want to talk about right now.

I fold my arms across my chest. "I'm just glad I'm away from him now."

"You don't have to worry about him anymore, Andy. You're with us now."

With them is right where I need to be.

## EIGHTEEN
## CASH

THE FIRST THING I do when we get back to the clubhouse is get the first aid kit out of the bathroom. Tommy and Pete are both standing around Slash, who is laying down on top of the bed.

I hand the first aid kit to Tommy, who takes a closer look at Slash's wound.

Tommy pours water over the wound and Slash grimaces in pain. "You're lucky this can be treated here instead of at the hospital. You already know it's going to hurt like hell when I stitch you up, so I don't need to warn you about that."

Slash grins. "Couldn't be any worse than getting stabbed in the chest."

I shake my head. "You're one tough bastard, Slash, and a great friend."

Pete leaves the room, and I join him in the living room. "We didn't find Liam at the hospital."

I am a tad bit disappointed hearing that, but we didn't expect him to be there. "I didn't find Laken either, but I want to keep looking for her."

Pete looks distant. "I hope we can find her today. I really do."

Something is wrong and I want to know what. "You can go ahead and tell me what's on your mind."

Pete gets out of his trance and looks at me. "I'm just thinking about my father, since today is the first time I've set foot in a hospital since he passed away. I wish that he was still around is all."

How the fuck could I forget that his father had passed away in a hospital?

"I'm sorry. My thoughts have just been of getting revenge on the people who have done this to Darcy."

When he speaks his voice is quiet. "You don't have anything to be sorry about, Cash. I'm the one who is sorry that we didn't find Liam. We found out that the Southern Demons are back here for selling drugs and gun trafficking."

"That's not the only thing they are back here for. This town must be a hotspot for a human trafficking ring and they are involved with that also. We've got to dismantle all of the shit they are getting stirred up before they get comfortable living here."

Pete looks at me, confused. "I always thought that Donald was weird, but would never expect to hear him running a human trafficking ring at his house."

"That's why we have to take a stand and let them know we don't appreciate them trying to take what is ours."

"I never did thank you for letting me stay here with Jaycee last night—" Pete starts to say but I interrupt him.

"You don't need to thank me. You deserved to have a good time."

Slash walks out of the bedroom with a liquor bottle in his hand. "I'm going home to take a bath. I'll be back as soon as I get out."

Pete gets up from the couch and follows Slash out the door. "I'm going with you. I need to get my clothes out of your truck."

Tommy comes out of the bedroom with an exhausted expression on his face. "My fun is over. Pam is here."

Shit.

She's the last person I expected to see today.

"What is she doing here?" I ask.

"Checking in on Darcy, so she can tell Rose how she is doing."

I hope Pam hasn't said or done anything to get on Darcy's nerves.

"I'm going to go check up on Darcy."

Tommy nods. "I'm staying here and calling my guys to see what I can find out. The last thing I want to hear is Pam's mouth running."

---

The parking lot is full at the grill so I don't bother stopping. Darcy will understand about me not stopping, because if I stop then I would be obligated to work. Working isn't something on my agenda today.

I look around me while riding back to my house. Now, more than ever before, it was time to be cautious, considering the Southern Demons are back in town. Who knows what the fuck they have up their sleeve.

I pass by several houses before finally making my way back into my neighborhood. I couldn't be more eager to talk to Darcy when I pull into my driveway. The few hours I was away from her made me worry about her because of the shape she was in this morning.

Darcy is sitting in the couch. I see her as soon as I walk

in the door. She grins at me through her pain. "I sure am glad to see you. I was wondering when you were going to come back home."

I press my lips against hers in a quick kiss, then sit down beside her. "The restaurant was busy so I didn't get you anything to eat, but I'll bring you some food in a little while."

She puts her fingers through mine and rests her head on my shoulder. "It's fine, babe. I'm still full from earlier."

I don't like seeing her up here all alone. "Where is everyone at?" I ask.

"Martin and Pam are in the basement."

Nancy comes out of the bedroom upstairs and looks at me. "You should have brought Darcy something to eat. It's not like Reapers Wings Bar and Grill is the only restaurant in town."

I roll my eyes. "Thank you for your input, Nancy. I appreciate it. Not that it is any concern to you, but I've been busy. Right now is the only chance I have had to stop by here all day."

Darcy sits up on the couch to look at Nancy. "I'm fine, Nancy. Really, there's no reason for anyone to get worked up right now."

Nancy doesn't accept that for an answer. "I'm not worked up, Darcy. I just don't understand how you can defend his actions. I don't see how you can sit here and act like it's okay when you know what he's about to do."

I try my hardest to remain calm. "Nancy, why do you always try to start shit with me? I can tell you right now I'm fucking sick of it. This is a part of who I am."

Nancy pinches her bottom lip and worry crosses her face. "This isn't a part of who you are, Cash, and I will never accept that. You used to be such a sweet and kind person, but now you're spiraling down a road of destruction. I don't even recognize the man who you are becoming anymore."

I stand up from the couch, fully prepared to make my way outside. "Are you kidding me right now, Nancy? A person that you don't even recognize? You were the one who raised me around this. How the fuck did you expect me to turn out?"

Darcy pulls at my shirt. "I love you and wouldn't want you to be anyone else."

I turn around and stare into Darcy's eyes. "Not now, sweetheart. This is between me and Nancy."

"I never wanted you to stay here, Cash." Nancy puts her face in her hands and then looks back at me. The agony is clear on her face. This is something that she's never told me before. It must be something she has been holding in for years. "I wish I could go back in time, because you and Rich would not be a part of this club."

Pam makes her way upstairs from the basement. "Where is Tommy at, Cash? I need to talk to him about a few things."

I speak to her in the calmest voice I can. "He's back at the clubhouse resting. We have a long day and night ahead of us. "

Pam gives me an understanding nod. "I'll just give him a call later."

"I'm selling my house, Cash," Nancy tells me. "I can't do this anymore."

Pam puts her hands on her hips. "Nancy, you are going to be making a big mistake if you sell your house. Just think about all of those grand babies that you will miss raising. You just need to calm down and think about what you are saying."

I can't do this anymore, so I push past them and go

outside. This is the exact reason why I can never have a conversation with Nancy. It always leads to her having something to say that I don't like. I am a thirty-five-year-old man who is capable of making his own decisions, whether they be good or bad.

Darcy sits down beside me on the steps. "You're not a bad person, Cash. If you were the two of us wouldn't be together. You do what's right for this town and club. These people here look up to you just like I do."

She always knows what to say to make me feel better. Just being around her makes me feel at ease and gives me peace of mind. It's a feeling that I can't describe and only a feeling I get when I'm around her.

I kiss her forehead. "Thank you for saying that, sweetheart. That's what makes everything worth it."

The door opens and Nancy walks outside. "This club is going to kill you, Cash. It already has. Your soul is damned straight to hell and that will never settle right with me. Don't you want to go heaven?"

I only state the obvious. "Nancy, I became the devil himself the minute you got together with my father so many years ago."

Nancy's hand collides with my cheek. It's worse than being stung by a bee. A bee means to bring you pain, not your own mother. "I loved your father more than anything in this world. He was a good man."

A good man that would commit murders and crimes.

I can't stand to hear another minute of this. "I am going to the clubhouse. I probably won't be back until later."

Darcy gives me a goodbye kiss. "Call me later so I know you're doing okay."

Nancy puts her hand over her mouth. "I'm sorry for the things that I said, Cash."

No, she isn't sorry for what she said. The only thing she is sorry about is me leaving so abruptly. "Goodbye, Nancy. I hope you find what you want living somewhere else."

I don't know where Nancy is planning on living but I'm not begging her to stay.

# NINETEEN
## DARCY

I AM ANNOYED that Cash left, all because he got into an argument with Nancy. But there isn't anything I can do about it now, other than hope he comes home later tonight. Sometimes I wish Nancy would just keep her mouth shut.

Martin steps out of the basement and glances around the room, searching for Cash. "Is Cash still here?"

I shake my head. "Him and Nancy got into it, so he left."

"Well, shit. I was wanting to talk him about a few things." Martin sits down on the couch and props up his feet. "I guess I will just call him later."

Pam gives me a hard look. It makes me uncomfortable, her staring at me. "What do you say about the two of us getting out of here?"

The last thing I want is for people to see my bruised face. "I can't go in anywhere."

"I wouldn't want you to go in anywhere. We can just drive around and talk," Pam replies.

I nod. "Okay. That sounds like a good idea to me."

It sounds like a hell of a good idea, because I don't want to be around Nancy.

Martin looks at Pam, then at me. "Do you two need an escort?"

Pam rolls her eyes. "Just stay here. We'll be back later."

———

I walk out the door before I can hear Martin's response and make myself comfortable in the passenger's seat.

It's a good thing Pam's windows are tinted and she has South Carolina tags. Nobody will be able to recognize me riding around with her.

Pam comes out of the house and starts the engine. There is silence in the car for several seconds. I don't know why, but she's taking her time creeping around the neighborhood. Finally, she starts talking. "How long has it been since you've talked to your mother and sister?"

I wasn't expecting to talk about my mother and sister with her. To be honest, I don't want to talk about them. I didn't want some big lecture from Pam telling me I need to go and see them.

I stare out the window and wish we weren't taking a car ride after all. "A couple of weeks ago. The two of them both seem to be doing fine."

Pam pulls over into the driveway of the house I grew up in. Nobody lives here now and the "for sale" sign is no longer in the yard. I haven't been inside of the house in a long time because it would open up old wounds. Wounds I don't need or want to open. "You know that I see your mother and Vanessa all the time. That little boy of Vanessa's is such a doll baby. I can't believe that you have never met him."

"I don't really think that me meeting him is any of your business."

She shakes her head at me in disapproval. "That's where you are wrong. It is my business. Your mother has been my best friend for years. If something bothers her, I can tell you very well that it bothers me."

Pam is right, because my mother and her go way back. The two of them had gone to school together long before they were married to members of the Reapers Wings. I remember Pam back then. She has changed a lot over the years. I guess being a Reapers Wings' old lady has made her tough and the bitch that she is now.

"She can come visit me any time. I don't understand why she won't."

It isn't like I'm the only one that can drive. Vanessa and Rose can both drive too. Better yet, they have cars. Pam is pointing the blame on me when the blame should be pointed towards all of us.

She doesn't believe a word I'm saying. I don't understand why she is so dead set on the two of us having this conversation. The worst part about it is that I can't leave. I am forced to stay in this car with her. She has me right where she wants me. "She doesn't come and visit you because she doesn't think you want her here."

I'm not surprised to hear that. The last time we had seen each other we had a fight. I was still living in Texas, barely making ends meet and still paying some of her bills. I told her I wasn't going to do it anymore and she got mad. I left and haven't seen her since.

"I'm fine with her coming for a few days and staying, but that's it."

"You need to make that clear the next time you talk to her. She's dying to see you."

I wouldn't necessarily say I'm dying to see her, but I do want to see her. It is the biggest reason why I want to plan a vacation to Sweetheart Bay, though that probably isn't going to happen now.

I fold my arms across my chest. "Is that why you wanted to go on this car ride?"

She shakes her head and lights a cigarette. "I wanted you to take a look at this house. You've still got things left inside. Things I don't think you should give up."

I left five years ago, as soon as my father had been buried. I hadn't been able to live with the pain of living here in this town anymore. I had felt so lost, like I was suffocating in my grief. When I left for Texas, the only thing that I had taken was a backpack full of clothes and necessities. I had left everything else behind.

I look at her, suddenly suspicious of her plans. "Does this house belong to you?"

She blows out smoke and I want a cigarette so damn bad I can hardly stand it. "No. It belongs to Tommy and he plans on selling it to your mother. They are going to be moving back here in a couple of months, whether you like it or not. I just want all of you to be on good terms with one another. I don't think that's too hard of a thing to ask."

It would be nice to have them so close, even though they will get on my nerves from time to time. Them moving back means I need to put the past behind me and start fresh with the two of them. Our relationship needs to be rekindled before it is too late.

The first thing that needs to be done is going through some of my things and reliving the wonderful memories. "I take it that since this house belongs to Tommy, you have the key." She finishes the rest of her cigarette and puts it in a cup. "Yeah, I do. That's the reason I came down here, to make sure you were doing okay. I just came in so I could tell your mother how you were doing."

I have a feeling she had gotten wind of me being beaten from Tommy. Her coming here makes perfect sense now. It wasn't to annoy the shit out of Martin. It was to go back and tell my mother what she knew about me. "Let's get this over with so we can get back. I'm starving."

"Cash should have gotten you food for lunch before he came and saw you."

"He doesn't like going to Reapers Wings Bar and Grill when it's busy. He feels like he's obligated to work. Today, of all days, he didn't want to because he has business to take care of concerning me."

"Then Nancy went and ran her mouth, so that put you on the back burner when it comes to food." She shakes her head at everything that is my life. "I'll tell you what. We can go to the grocery store and I can fix the two of us something. We don't need all of that greasy shit from Reapers Wings Bar and Grill anyway."

"That sounds like a great idea to me."

Pam has always been a nosy woman, so I shouldn't expect anything different from her now. "So, tell me who is it that did this to you?"

"This girl named Laken Head, Hank, and Liam." I continue walking up the driveway and stop so that she can put the key in the door. "Liam is the only one I've never seen before."

She stops herself from putting the key in the door at the mention of Hank's name. "Somebody should have done away with Hank a long time ago. Me and everyone else hates his fucking guts. The old, perverted piece of shit didn't rape you, did he?"

I can't help but feel uncomfortable talking to her about

this. "No, thank God. He didn't. I bit his tongue before he had a chance to do anything."

She unlocks the door and the first thing that I see when walking in the door is the old couch in the living room. There isn't anything special about the couch. It's blue and was brand new when my daddy had bought it.

"He probably got angry. So that's why your face looks like it does."

I nod. "It hurt like hell, but it was worth not being raped."

"I'm proud of you for sticking up for yourself, even if you did suffer the consequences."

"It was awful. I hope to God that is never happens again."

She raises her eyebrows and gives my shoulder a squeeze. "I'm just glad they didn't kill you, that Cash got to you in time."

"He wouldn't have gotten to me if it wasn't for this woman, Andy." Thinking about Andy now makes me want to cry. There wasn't a chance in hell I was ever going to see her again. "She was my roommate when I lived in Texas and the person responsible for saving my life."

"I see everything clearly now. I'm glad you told me about everything that happened."

I sit down on the couch and the memories of my father come rushing back at once. "I can't believe you guys didn't get rid of anything."

"This stuff doesn't belong to us. It belongs to you, Vanessa, and Rose. If anything is going, you all will be the one tossing things out."

"His death must have been a painful thing for my mother to just get up and leave, since all of her stuff is still here. It makes me feel bad for leaving. I should have told her where I was going."

"To be honest, Darcy, the worst pain was knowing she had lost you too."

Regret and remorse tug at my gut for treating Vanessa and my mother like I had. I should have stayed and dealt with my pain along with them. Then the three of us could have moved to Sweetheart Bay to start our lives over.

Instead, I had chosen to get away from the club and everybody I knew. I had wanted to live my own life without knowing anyone. It sure wasn't what it was cracked up to be. The first couple of months I lived in Texas, my car was my home. I didn't have money saved up to cover rent. One night, after I had gotten off of work, a man tried to attack me but Andy stopped him. She realized I was living in my car and ushered me inside her one-bedroom apartment. The two of us have been friends ever since.

"Him dying so suddenly filled me with so much pain that I couldn't bear to stay here in this town anymore. I wanted to walk away. I thought walking away would numb the pain, but instead it made things so much worse."

"It's hard when people die, but that doesn't mean we should shut people out of our life." Her first husband, Martin's father Leo, had passed away when we were just kids. He had died of cirrhosis of the liver. "Instead, we let them carry some of our pain with us."

I walk into the kitchen and remember the last day my father was still alive. He had taken to fixing me the one thing I love, biscuits and gravy. His gravy was always the best because he got it just right. It was never too thin or runny. Before he had left the house, he'd given me a hug and told me he loved me. I had told him I loved him too, and that was the last time the two of us exchanged words.

The tears I have been holding in for so long fall down my face. The only thing that I want in this world is to see my father. But I can't see him or talk to him because he's not coming back.

Pam comes over to me and rubs my back. "I knew that was coming. You need to get it all out. Cry as much as you need to. I'm not going anywhere. I'll be right here with you."

Her words are comforting to me and for the first time that she has made a surprise visit in I am glad she is here, even if she could be a little nicer than she is. She just understands me in a way that no one here has before.

I sniffle and reach for the tissue that is on the table beside me. "After all this time, I never knew Tommy had bought this house. It wasn't anything Cash or anybody else told me."

"Nobody told you because that was a wound they didn't want to open."

"I miss him so much. The pain is almost unbearable." The two of us had been so close. He was the man I could talk to about anything and everything. He would always take time to listen to what I had to say. "The thing that hurts the most is that I never got a chance to say goodbye."

A wave of sadness creeps over her face. "Martin's father was an alcoholic and drunk himself to death. It's the reason I have never found an interest in drinking. He was only forty when he died and his death broke Martin's heart more than it did mine. I'm glad I got the chance to tell him goodbye, but his death will always hurt."

"I'm sorry about your husband."

"I am, too. He was a good man who died way too soon."

I wince in pain when I stand up. It's time to go into my bedroom. I walk back through the living room, past the bathroom, and into my bedroom. I wish I was back in my twenties again without a worry in the world.

The ring on the night stand catches my eye, so I pick it up and examine it. It has the Reapers Wings emblem on it, a skull wearing a hoodie with angel wings around it. The ring belonged to my father, but I hadn't left it here. Pam or Tommy probably did. I am definitely going to take it back home with me. It would be something I cherish for the rest of my life.

"I was hoping that ring would be something you would find." Pam leans in the doorway of the bedroom with a small smile on her face. "Rose and Vanessa both wanted you to have it."

"Thank you for bringing me here. It means a lot to me."

She nods. "It's something you should have done a hell of a long time ago."

I ask the question, because I hope the answer is sooner rather than later. "Do you know the exact month Vanessa and Rose are moving back?"

"We haven't worked out all of those details yet, but before there is snow on the ground."

There is still plenty of time for me to see them before then. Winter isn't that far away, only a couple of months, and I can live with that.

## TWENTY
# CASH

I HAD to leave and go to the clubhouse to clear my head. I didn't need to listen to Nancy's bullshit. Yeah, she is my mother, but she has no right to mess around with the thoughts going on in my head. She doesn't have a right to weigh in on my conscience. That's the reason I can't stand to be around her.

Heath is talking to Tommy when I walk in the door. "I was just telling Tommy that five teens have gone missing from Sweetheart Bay in the last couple of weeks. Authorities don't have any leads or know what's going on."

Heath never stays long when he does come over. He always has a lot of business to take care of as the sheriff. I trust him with my life and know he will never turn on the club. He's the only person in this county I can say that about.

I sit down on the bar stool beside him. "That's something great to come home from vacation too."

Heath snorts. "It wasn't much of a vacation, I'll tell you that."

"Speaking of vacations. I could use one away from Pam," Tommy chimes in.

I snicker. "You'll get a vacation from her when you're dead."

Heath shows me the flyer that's in his hand. "This girl went missing yesterday. From my understanding, she went missing on her way to work in broad daylight. There are no witnesses who saw anything and no one is coming forward with information."

I take a closer look at the flyer. The girl appears to be a teenager, no older than seventeen. She has long, red hair and blue eyes. Her name is Sidney Eagle. "I can't say I have seen her. Looking at her doesn't ring any bells. I have a good idea where she could be, though, and that's Donald's house. The Southern Demons are back in town and are holding at least one girl there that we know of."

Heath sticks the flyer back in his pocket. "Tommy told me about what happened at Donald's house. We need to go in there when your crew gets back, see what we can find out. Chances are they will be long gone by then, but if they are holding a lot of girls, they can't have gone far."

"I talked to Cole a little while ago and they were getting ready to leave." Tommy stands up to stretch out his legs. "They won't be here until midnight at the earliest, and that's if they don't run into trouble."

"It doesn't matter what time they come in. We are going in there tonight without any questions being asked," Heath says. "This shit needs to be shut down before it even gets started."

"We are trying to find Laken Head. Do you know where she would be?" I ask.

"I've seen her at the abandoned cabin on the outskirts of town more times than I care to remember." Heath gets up and walks towards the door. "Call me and let me know when all of the boys are here. I'll be waiting. I'm sorry about what happened to Darcy, Cash."

I nod. "Thank you. We will be in touch."

---

I head outside, eager to get this show on the road. I watch Heath pull out of the driveway and Tommy joins me. "I hope Slash and Pete come back soon so we can get going."

"I'm sure they will." Tommy takes out a pack of cigarettes and lights one. "I know you're impatient. I would be too if I was taking a walk in your shoes. Don't let what happened to Darcy eat you up inside, or a wedge will form between the two of you."

Tommy always has a way of knowing what I am thinking even before I say it. "How can I do that, Tommy, when this was clearly my fault? I should have been paying attention, but instead, I let my guard down."

He takes a few puffs off of his cigarette. "Just because it was your fault doesn't mean you live with that guilt forever. You learn to accept what happened and love her the best way you can. The last thing you need to do is let them destroy your relationship, because then they will have won."

Rage comes to the surface, knowing the pain Darcy had experienced was all too real. She will always have to live with that trauma and it infuriates me. Liam, Laken, and Hank are all going to get what is coming to them. I can't wait to get my revenge. Then I won't let the guilt of what happened get the best of me. "Laken had her hands wrapped around Darcy's neck last night when I walked in the door. That's where the guilt kicks in. I need that fucking junkie dead today."

Seeing that image of Darcy will forever haunt me for the rest of my life.

He takes the last few puffs of his cigarette and rubs my back with his hand. "I want to tell you about something that happened way before you were ever born."

I let out a deep breath and try not to let the rage consume me. "I'm all ears, Tommy."

"I was set to marry the love of my life at the age of twenty-five. I loved that woman more than anything in this world. The Southern Demons had made their presence known in Sweetheart Bay and they attacked her. They left her for dead because they had beaten her so bad. She landed herself in the hospital and was on a ventilator for a couple of weeks. I let my anger get the best of me and made the worst decision of my life. I let her go the minute she got out of that hospital."

"I take it that's the reason you didn't get married again until ten years ago."

"I couldn't let myself get that close to a woman again before Pam. I lived with anger and guilt all of those years, even got myself put in prison for stupid shit. But when I met Pam, we instantly hit it off. She knows what club life is all about and how to defend and take care of herself. I love her, but hot damn, she gets on my nerves sometimes."

I laugh. Pam has a way of getting on everyone's nerves. I can't imagine being married to her. "At least you did manage to get somewhat of a happily ever after."

"I did get a happily ever after, but Pam isn't the love of my life. The girl from so many years ago was. I shouldn't have let her go. Don't you ever let your anger get you that far, because I regret not holding onto her."

"You don't have anything to worry about, Tommy. My

life would be nothing without Darcy. I refuse to live life without her, because I just can't."

He grins. "Be sure to invite me to the wedding."

Slash comes rolling up on his motorcycle. "Something must have happened or went down for the two of you to be standing out here like this. I'm sorry it took us so long. Lover Boy decided to take a long ass hot shower."

Pete rolls his eyes. "My shower wasn't anything compared to your bath."

"We are heading out towards the cabin at Screaming Cats." I put on my helmet, then crank up my motorcycle. "Heath claims Laken hangs out there, so let's get going because Heath needs us later tonight."

Pete looks confused. "What does he need us for? I have plans with Jaycee tonight and don't want to not show up."

"We are going to be going into Donald's house," Tommy answers, "but I'm sure that won't be until midnight."

Pete's face lightens up. "Sounds pretty fucking good to me. As long I'm able to get a piece of ass, I'll be doing okay."

I shake my head. "I'm just glad you had a good time last night."

Pete nods. "Let's go. If I recall correctly, you said you need blood on your hands."

---

Screaming Cats is the smallest town in Heartwood County, with a population of only five hundred. There's nothing much to do over there. It's not a popular place to go.

The cabin is off to itself, a place for people to go to hang out and do drugs. People flock to it since no one lives there and the cabin is still in great condition. The man who the cabin belonged to died a couple of months ago in a hunting accident.

An old black car is parked outside. I don't know who the vehicle belongs to, but I am about to find out. As soon as I park my motorcycle, I walk towards the cabin.

I hear Tommy and Pete pull up behind Slash, but I don't bother looking back or waiting on them.

I don't knock on the cabin door. I just barge inside. A woman I don't recognize is in the living room snorting pills. She looks alarmed, so I hold my hands out.

"I'm not looking to do you any harm." I talk nice and calmly, even though I want to scream at her. "I'm just looking for somebody and was wondering if you had seen her."

The woman shakes her head at me uneasily. "There's been nobody up here but me for a couple of days. I don't want no part in what you're going to do to anybody. I just want to be in peace, so please leave."

Laken must have told her something or she wouldn't be talking to me like this.

I get a twenty-dollar bill out of my pocket in hopes of persuading her to talk. "Are you sure you don't know where Laken Head is?"

Slash comes in the door. "I take it that Laken probably isn't here."

Before I have a chance to respond, the woman takes off running through the house and out the back door. This was the thing I was afraid of happening, but on the bright side, there are more of us than her.

I see Pete running after her through the window inside and he's gaining speed. It is a good thing that he's not a smoker or he would never be able to catch her at the rate she is running. "She knows something, Slash."

"We'll get it out of her."

I stroll outside and join Tommy. Pete grabs ahold of the girl and she is kicking her feet trying to get free. "Quit moving. It's not like I'm going to kill you," Pete says.

The woman jerks her arms, trying to break free, but Pete's grip is unbreakable. She thrashes around, and with a roll of his eyes, Pete whips his pistol across her face to get her to calm down. If only she would have answered me truthfully to begin with, this never would have happened.

The woman holds onto her face when she joins us. It is such a shame there is going to be a bruise on her cheekbone. "Laken gave me the drugs and then left. That's all I know. I swear to you. Please don't hurt me. I just came up here to get high."

The fact that she mentions Laken infuriates me. This junkie deserves to die for lying to me.

I get out my gun and press it against her forehead. "There is more to the fucking story than what you are telling me, so I suggest you start talking. All it will take is one bullet to blow your fucking head off!"

She begins to cry, but that doesn't matter to me. "All I know is she had plans to leave. I'm sorry. I really don't know anything else."

I place my finger inches away from the trigger. "You tell me where she went, then I will leave you alone and pretend this never happened."

Her entire body shakes in fear. "I swear on my life, I don't know. If I knew, I would tell you."

Her bullshit lies eat at my nerves. I had come here wanting revenge, but instead I'm stuck with this junkie. It would be so easy for me to pull the trigger when it comes to her. So fucking easy. I am going to do it. I inch my way towards the trigger.

Slash strolls towards me. "Cash, let her go. She told us what she knew."

Tommy rams into me, tackling me to the ground. The gun flies across the ground and lands at Pete's feet. "Cash, get ahold of yourself. This woman here didn't do anything to you. Just let it go and let her be."

Pete looks at the woman, who is no longer within my grasp. "Get the fuck out of here and I mean now!"

I slam my fist into Tommy's face. He doesn't know if this woman knows more than she is letting on. She could know everything and we just let her go for no good reason.

Slash puts me in a headlock, his forearm pressing against my throat. I gasp for air, but can't manage to get it in my lungs. Pressure builds in my face as I claw at his arms. "Think about this, Cash. This is not who you are. We came here for Laken and no one else. You are better than this, brother."

I hold my hands up in the air and Slash loosens his grip. "I promise. I'm done. You can let me go."

Slash lets me go. "Don't make me regret this."

Tommy's fist hits me and it brings me back into reality. "Pete isn't the only one with anger issues. I didn't realize that you did, too. Son of a fucking bitch, you know how to punch."

"Let's get out of here and go back to the club house to regroup," I reply. "I need a clear head to think before we go out searching for her later."

A man walks out of the cabin with a gun in his hand. He fires his gun in the air, showing us he means business. "I would suggest you all get the hell out of here. You've done enough damage."

I look at Tommy and whisper. "You should have just let me kill her."

Tommy rolls his eyes. "That wouldn't have done any good. We would have this guy to deal with then."

He knows as well as I do that this guy is going to let us leave in one piece.

Slash gets up from his position behind a tree. "I'll be damned if that's not you, Bruise Lawson."

Bruise lowers the shotgun and jumps off the porch. "Eddie, my man. I haven't seen you in years. I heard about your boy a little while ago. Didn't think you were still around these parts."

"Do you mind filling us in with how you two know each other?" I ask.

"Bruise here was my right-hand man when I use to burglarize houses as a teenager," Slash informs me.

Was there a time in his life when he wasn't a criminal?

Bruise starts rolling with laughter. "Those were some good times we had. I sure wish I could go back and relive them."

"Is that girl your girlfriend or something?" Pete asks.

Bruise is still laughing. "That girl doesn't mean nothing to me. I just brought her up here to get high with her and get a little pussy, that's all."

Slash takes a good look at Bruise. "Have you seen Laken Head? We are looking for her. We came up here in hopes of finding her."

Bruise shakes his head. "I haven't seen her. I promise you that I'd tell you if I did."

Slash asks the question one more time. "Are you sure you haven't seen her?"

"I swear to you, I haven't seen her. I wouldn't lie to you now, Eddie. I have no reason to lie or stand in your way."

"I guess we are going to be getting on our way then." Slash hops on his motorcycle and gets ready to ride. "It was nice talking to you, Bruise. I guess I will be seeing you around."

Bruise nods. "You sure as hell will be seeing me around if I'm not in jail."

I hop onto my own motorcycle, disappointed. "Do you believe him?"

Slash cranks up his motorcycle. "To be honest, Cash, I don't know what to believe. He's changed over the years. I've never known him to do drugs. The two of us used to get drunk every weekend and break into houses. That's it."

"I guess that what you're saying is it's not worth getting it out of him."

"I promise you, Cash, you will find her, even if you don't today."

The worst thing about him saying that is quite frankly, I'm not so sure.

# TWENTY-ONE

# DARCY

PAM DECIDED TO MAKE SPAGHETTI, since it's something quick and easy to make. The two of us were both starving by the time we got finished at the old house. It made me just a tad bit disappointed that Cash hadn't bought me lunch, but I could understand his reasoning.

For the first time since we have been back, Nancy comes into the kitchen where Pam has just finished cooking. "I didn't mean to upset Cash earlier. I'm sorry if I bothered you."

I have a mouthful of spaghetti. "It's fine, Nancy. I understand your worry when it comes to him. I do think that you need to realize the person that he is and come to terms with that."

Pam has her back to the two of us while she makes herself a plate of food. "You should have never said anything, Nancy. Our sons are grown and need to make their own decisions. They need to live their life the way they want to live it."

Nancy folds her arms across her chest. "I don't think

that's fair to say, Pam, not when my son is heading down a path of destruction."

Pam sits down at the table in front of me with her plate and fork in her hands. "It's not your job to convert him to Christianity and make him go to church. If you don't stop, he's going to end up hating you forever."

Nancy lets out a sigh of frustration. "I just wish he could see that he doesn't have to live life this way."

"Nancy, you're a good person, but don't try to talk him out of leaving this club." I take another bite of my food and wash it down with water. "He's never going to leave it. It's a part of who he is and has always been."

Nancy fixes a plate and then sits down at the table with the two of us. I thought that since we weren't telling her what she wanted to hear, this would be the last place she wanted to be. "I guess I've just been thinking ahead when I think of this life. I just want to see my two sons join me in Heaven. Is that too much to ask?"

Pam takes a sip of her tea. "I think that you need to stop being so religious and just think about this life we are in right now. I believe in Heaven and Hell as much as you do, but it's not something our boys want to hear."

I can't believe the three of us are all sitting down, talking, and not having arguments with one another. The air is clear between the three of us and it's peaceful. "I have to say, I agree with Pam. Cash won't even talk about God with me."

Nancy nods. "I guess the only thing I can do is pray for him and hope he finds God before it's too late."

"That's the only way to do things, Nancy. It's what I do." Pam picks up a paper towel off the table and wipes the sauce from her mouth. "You know, Nancy, the two of us are more alike than you think."

I finish off the rest of the spaghetti and dig into the salad. "I do know one thing. The two of you both know how to cook."

Nancy forces a smile. "What can I say? Pam taught me everything I know about cooking. She cooked for us all the time when I was just a little girl."

Pam shakes her head. "Now, Nancy, I am only eight years older than you. The both of us were still little. I just didn't like the fact that I spent all of my time taking care of you, since mommy died right before your second birthday."

Nancy's face quickly turns from a smile into a wave of sadness. I imagine thinking back on the memories did that to her. It makes me realize just how lucky I am to have my mother and that she is still alive. "I would do anything to have been able to know her."

"What happened to your mother?" I ask.

"She died in a car crash after taking me to school," Pam answers.

That is absolutely horrible and something I hadn't known about the two of them. It makes me sad to hear them speak of it now. I couldn't imagine losing Rose at such a young age, or at all, even if the two of us have never been all that close.

Nancy takes a bite of her spaghetti and chews it up before speaking. "That's how the two of us got associated with the club. Our father was a member. Most of our days and nights were spent there, even though that was no place for a child to be."

Pam rolls her eyes. "It could have been a lot worse though, Nancy. He could have given us away, but he didn't. Daddy was a good man and you can't say he wasn't. He kept food in the house for us so I could cook, and kept a roof over our head. So being at the club house really wasn't nothing."

I don't know whether I side with Pam or not in this matter. I wouldn't have been too keen on having children at the club house all of the time, not with the way they partied, but things could have been different back then. "Did the two of you have a babysitter?" I hoped they did because they had been so young.

"Your mother, Rose, was our baby sitter." Nancy speaks so soft, more like herself. "That's how we became friends with your mom, how we got to know her. Talk about a good cook. Your mother has always been a great one."

I never did know that. She never mentioned it. The two of us have a lot of catching up to do and a lot to talk about. I am going to have to plan a trip down there and see her when I wasn't so banged up.

Pam finishes off the rest of her spaghetti and stands up from the table. She sets her plate in the sink, then turns around to look at Nancy. "I've always been jealous of you, Nancy. That's the reason I don't talk to you much. It's never had anything to do with Christianity. I am jealous of you because you got two sons and I only had one."

Nancy clears her throat before she speaks. "I'm sorry that you weren't able to have more children, Pam. I know how much those miscarriages must have hurt, plus losing Leo when you did."

"I am sorry, Nancy, for the way that I have treated you over the years." Pam dabs at her eyes with a paper towel. "It wasn't right of me when you yourself didn't have the picture-perfect life either."

Nancy gets up from the table and gives Pam a hug. After all of these years, the two of them are finally making up. "There's no need for an apology, Pam. Let's just get over the past and move on."

Martin, who has been asleep down in the basement,

appears in the hallway. "I don't know what's got into you, Pam, to let Nancy give you a hug." He walks over to the stove to make himself a plate. "I must have really missed something."

Pam pulls apart from Nancy and looks over at Martin. "You should have gone with the guys. You know very well that I never go anywhere without my gun. I will be staying here a couple of days anyway, just to see what you've been into."

Martin shakes his head. "Why am I not surprised that you're staying here awhile?"

Pam puts her hand on her hip. "You're lucky I'm still alive. I don't think that it's the end of the world, since I'm here to keep you from drinking so damn much."

Nancy leaves the kitchen and goes to the door. "I think I'm going to go home and lay down. I will see you guys later. The spaghetti was delicious, Pam."

Pam nods. "I'll be coming over later so that the two of us can talk more."

"You're more than welcome in my house any time," Nancy says before going out the door.

Martin takes out a beer from the fridge and carries it into the living room. "You're not going to stop me from drinking, Pam, so I don't even want to hear it from you. There's nothing wrong with a beer every now and then."

The expression on Pam's face has *bitch* written all over it. "I know you drink every single day. That's how your father died, because he was an alcoholic. If you want to throw your life away you go right ahead, but it makes you a stupid little shit."

"How can you say that to me, when the last thing that I am is like Dad?"

I go into my bedroom and shut the door behind me. I get

out my cell phone and do the thing I have been wanting to do all day. There isn't any reason for me to put it off anymore. I dial Rose's number and she answers on the first ring. "Darcy, is that you? I've been waiting for you to call."

It feels so good to hear my mother's voice after weeks of not talking to her. I can't wait to visit and see her in person. "Pam's here. I just wanted to see how you were doing. She showed me Daddy's ring and I want to thank you for letting me have it. I'm sorry I left when I did five years ago. I didn't realize how much you were hurting, too."

"Oh Darcy, you and your father were always close. I couldn't think of a better person to have that ring besides you." There is silence on the phone for several seconds and I hear a baby crying, probably my nephew. "I always knew you would come back and get together with Cash. I'm just surprised it took you two so long. Speaking of Cash, I hope that he's treating you well."

"He's treating me just fine, but something happened." Tears form in my eyes and I let them fall. I hate being emotional on the phone especially, but I can't help it because I need to talk to her. "I was beaten, Mommy, almost killed. I won't be able to get out of the house for a little while."

"Oh my goodness gracious, Darcy, that is just horrible." She sounds absolutely shocked that something so horrible happened to me. "I promise I will come visit with you as soon as I can. I miss you something awful."

I wipe the tears away with my hand. "I miss you and Vanessa both too. I can't wait to get my hands on little Brenton, since I've never seen him before."

"It's so good to hear your voice, but I better get off here now." I don't want her to go but I know that she has to. "I need to give Brenton a bottle and put him down for a nap.

Vanessa went out with some of her friends and put me on babysitting duty."

That sounds like something Vanessa would do.

"I love you, Mommy. Goodbye for now."

"I love you, my sweet girl. Goodbye."

———

I grab the ring that is sitting on the nightstand. I am going to have to buy a necklace chain so that I can wear it every day. I miss my father so much that a hole is in my heart. A hole that can never be filled.

Pam and Martin must have finished arguing, because I don't hear them anymore.

There is a knock on the door, followed by Martin's voice. "Can I come in there to talk to you a minute?"

I wonder what this is about. "I don't mind. Come on in."

He comes in and sits down on my bed. "Cash called me when you and Pam were gone. They didn't find Laken. He doesn't think that they are going to find her today, but it's not set in stone."

I'm not worried about Laken because I know she will show up eventually. "I hope Cash doesn't stay at the club house tonight if he doesn't get the job done."

I don't want to be alone tonight. I want him here with me whether he kills her or not. I have spent most of the day without him and need to snuggle up to him tonight.

"If he stays at the club house, I know that I won't be going anywhere."

He's telling me something I already know.

"I hope that he comes back so that you can get some relief."

"I love it here, if we are being honest." I thought being at the clubhouse was his favorite place to be, but I guess even that got old after a while. "It's quiet here, a place that I can relax."

"You're more than welcome to stay here any time."

He gets up from the bed and stands in the doorway. "I'll definitely keep that in mind."

"Pam just wants what's best for you. You know that, right?"

He nods. "Yeah, I do know that, but it doesn't stop her from being a pain in my ass."

TWENTY-TWO
# CASH

WHEN WE REACH the bottom of the hill, four Southern Demons are waiting for us. They are in the middle of the road, making it impossible to get around them. It makes me wonder why they are here. Have they been watching us this entire time?

Hugh stands in the front, and when he sees me, he speaks. "I'm sad to hear that Darcy isn't dead. I was sure we were going to kill her yesterday."

I grab my gun and point it at him. "Nothing is stopping me from killing you right now. You are nothing but a pathetic human being who is going to pay for everything you have done."

The minute that I pulled out my gun, everyone else does too. If the guns are fired, then there is a good chance all of us will come out of here injured or dead.

"I'm not going to pay for anything, Cash. That will be you." Hugh sounds so sure of himself. "You're going to pay for hiding Andy, for taking her away from me. She's mine and belongs to no one except me."

My rage boils over and I am close to becoming undone. I

am so close to ending Hugh's life right now. I don't give a damn that he works for the drug cartel. That doesn't make a difference to me. The only thing I can think about is what happened to Darcy. Everything that happened to her was all because of him. "Andy is no longer yours, so stop thinking that she is, you controlling psychotic pig."

"Oh, but she will always be mine. I will never stop looking." Hugh smirks at me like the evil monster he is. "We already know that she's in Sweetheart Bay, and it won't be long until we pinpoint her exact location."

Tommy grabs onto my shirt and whispers in my ear. "Stay calm and cool. The last thing we need is for our bodies to be laying in the road. Put the gun back in your pants and just listen to what this bastard has to say."

It takes everything inside of me to do what Tommy says. "Are you just here to threaten me? Because this territory belongs to the Reapers Wings and always has. Nothing about that will ever change, so don't you for a fucking moment think that it will."

Hugh stares at me for a second before answering. "I know everything about all of you. I've been watching you for months." He turns to Slash, who is standing beside me. "You have a sweet little girl, Slash, who is all grown up. I sure would hate to see what happens to her when you're not around."

Slash takes a lunge at Hugh, but I hold him back. "What the fuck is wrong with you? I wouldn't even think about doing anything to your family even though I hate your fucking guts. Hell, I hate all of your fucking guts, but this is just between us. There's no need to bring our families into it."

Hugh throws his head back and laughs. "That's where you are wrong. Bringing families into this just makes things so much more fun. It gets my point across and lets you know that I am in control."

I glare at Hugh. "There will be a day when I take my time killing you. I will enjoy it when you scream bloody murder."

Hugh lets out a sigh and shakes his head. "That's not going to happen. There are more of us than there are of you. Our numbers are growing each and every single day, because we find pride in our heritage."

Slash spits at Hugh's feet. "You must be living in some daydream if you think things are going to go back to the way they used to be. Segregation is never going to happen, so you might as well get that out of your stupid fucking head."

Hugh stares intently in Slash's eyes. "You would be thrown out of the Southern Demons club in a heartbeat. I do not know what kind of club you all think you are running. It's a joke if you ask me, letting colored folks join and mixing in with all of you."

The more I hear Hugh talk, the more I want to put a bullet in his head. "We are a club where the color of anyone's skin doesn't matter. You need to get with the times, Hugh, because racism should have been over a long time ago."

Hugh sounds serious when he speaks. "I am watching every single move that you all make. The next time I see you, we aren't going to be having a friendly conversation, because you'll be dead in your grave."

"Not if we kill you first," I answer.

Hugh doesn't say another word to me. He gets on his motorcycle and leaves. His guys follow him out.

Pete, who hasn't said anything, finally speaks. "Bruise or that girl has to be working for the Southern Demons. There is no way that they would know we were coming here."

"Let's just go to the clubhouse to regroup," Tommy suggests. "We need to settle our nerves and think about what to do next."

I'm more than ready to blow someone's head off.

———

Rage ignites the monster inside of me and I can't see straight. Hugh was there right before my eyes and I didn't put a bullet in his head. He was the person who had ordered the hit on Darcy and no one else.

I grab a bottle of liquor from the refrigerator and throw it against the wall. The glass and liquor shatter everywhere, but it gets rid of some of my steam.

I was more than ready to kill Laken for the role she played in what happened to Darcy. I hate every single thing about her. I want her dead. She doesn't deserve to be living on this earth anymore. Her hands were wrapped around Darcy's neck when I had found her. She is the person who would have ended her life if I hadn't gotten there in time. That's why she's the person I want dead today.

Slash is sitting at the bar. "We tried, Cash, and she wasn't at the cabin. There's nothing else we can do about that right now."

"I don't accept that answer, Slash." I am on the brink of insanity. "I can't accept that answer, Slash. Not when Darcy is counting on me to get the job done today. The last thing I want to do is let her down."

"Darcy won't be upset, Cash. She'll understand."

I don't want to believe him, even though he's right. "I just was so sure this was going to be easy."

Instead, it was fucking hard, all because I didn't have

any more leads. Nobody else had the slightest clue where she was or could be.

"You and I both know murdering people isn't easy." Slash lights up a cigarette and opens a beer. "It takes time to plan everything out and for things to fall into place like they are supposed to. Just relax, Cash. You have me all stressed out. I am worried about what you are going to do next. I am starting to think you are the one I need to watch, not Pete."

I slap myself in the face, trying to get ahold of my emotions. *It's not the end of the world that you didn't find Laken yet. Everything will be okay, because you will never stop searching for her. Just imagine how bittersweet it will be whenever you pull the trigger. How proud that will make Darcy, when Laken is dead.*

*Darcy being so traumatized by what happened last night brings fuel to the fire. I need to find Laken so I can blow her fucking head off. Then all will be good in the world, since she will be fucking dead. I will laugh my ass off about killing her, since nothing is sweeter than revenge. I just can't fucking find her and it's killing me on the inside!*

I let out a scream in frustration, then get a beer out of the fridge. "I can't believe that I just let Hugh walk away. I could have put a bullet in his head and I should have."

"No, you shouldn't have, because we don't know how many people we are up against." Slash takes a swig of his beer. It's the first time in a long time I've seen him look like hell. Getting grazed by that bullet earlier had really done a number on him. "We need to find out more about Hugh and the cartel he works for before we kill him."

Tommy comes out of the bathroom and has a seat on the bar stool. "I just got word from Jamie. He's told me a few things we need to know." Jamie is the vice president at Sweetheart Bay and one of the best people when it comes to computers. "Hugh is working for the Smith family, a family who lives on the outskirts of Sweetheart Bay."

"Why the fuck would they come back here, of all places?" Slash asks.

"Because it makes perfect sense for Hugh and the Southern Demons to set up here. Think about it, Slash. Down here there isn't any competition. They can be suppliers and make all the money they want, if we let them," I explain.

The Southern Demons have competition in Sweetheart Bay when it comes to dealing drugs. Over twenty years ago, the Reapers Wings formed an agreement with the Devil's Monsters. An agreement was made that the south side of Sweetheart Bay belongs to the Devil's Monsters and the north side belongs to the Reapers Wings. In that agreement, the Devil's Monsters aren't allowed to bring drugs in on the Reapers Wings side and the Reapers Wings aren't allowed to sell guns on the Devil's Monsters side.

Not only had the Reapers Wings formed an agreement with the Devil's Monsters, but we are allies too. We always have each other's back and look out for each other.

Slash takes a long sip of his beer. "The better question is where would they set up in this county? It can't be somewhere obvious or we would have found out about them before now."

I wonder the exact same thing. That's the reason we have to go looking later.

Pete comes out of his bedroom and sits down on a couch. "Hugh could have been all talk about their numbers growing. I don't see how anyone in their right fucking mind would want to become a Southern Demons."

I light a cigarette and blow out smoke. "I don't see how anyone could be a Southern Demons either, brother. It makes me sick knowing everything they stand for. This world is made for everyone, regardless of our skin color."

Slash drinks the rest of his beer and then heads to the fridge for another one. "You all know I'm no pussy, but my shoulder hurts like hell. I need to sit here and drink a couple of beers before we go anywhere else."

I blow out smoke and my concern for Slash grows. "I can get ahold of Melvin so he can get you some antibiotics."

Melvin, the doctor in town, supplies the club with whatever medication we need. He was a friend of my father's and has always been loyal to the club, even after my father's death.

Slash sits back down at the bar and opens up the bottle of beer. "I would rather drink me a couple of beers. It'll help numb the pain."

Tommy looks at Slash like he's crazy. "That shit is going to get infected if you don't take care of yourself. Cash, get a hold of Melvin to get this dumb ass some antibiotics before he ends up in the hospital. Sometimes I think you all are lacking common sense. Good fucking grief."

I blow out smoke and laugh. "I'm going to go home to see Darcy, since I won't be staying with her tonight."

Slash grins like he's proud of me. "When you get back, we can go out looking for Laken some more. Just give me a couple of hours and then I'll be alright."

Tommy slaps me hard on the back. "I see you've been thinking about what we talked about earlier. Go be with Darcy for a little while and then we can go back out."

It is disappointing I haven't found Laken, but being home right now with Darcy is right where I need to be.

TWENTY-THREE
# PETE

I FIGURED I would go to Jaycee's an hour early since Cash hasn't come back from his house yet. I hate that we weren't able to find Laken, but the night is still young. We could still possibly find her, and if we can't tonight, there will always be tomorrow.

I go up to Jaycee's door and knock but there is no answer. Her car is parked in the driveway so I know she's inside. I peek inside the window and don't see her in the living room. I put my hand on the door handle to see if it's unlocked. It is.

I step inside and her cat Precious greets me. The cat rubs against my legs and I bend down to pet it. "Jaycee, I'm here. I thought I would come a little early."

"I just got finished doing my hair and will be right there!" She calls from a bedroom down the hall. "Feel free to make yourself at home. I have plenty of beer in the fridge."

I sit down on the couch, not particularly interested in drinking right now. The thing I am interested in is seeing her. "I'll just be petting Precious!"

The cat gets up on my lap, purring away. I've never known a cat to be so sweet, especially when it comes to strangers.

Several seconds later she appears and damn she looks hot. Her brown hair is straight and she is wearing a cute little short dress. Makeup is on her face and she cleans up good. This was a nice refresher from seeing her at the restaurant.

I whistle at her. "Damn, you look nice."

She grins. "All I've been thinking about is you coming over tonight."

"There's nowhere else I would rather be than here spending time with you."

She reaches out her hand and I grab hold of it. "Come on. The food should be finished now."

I follow her into the kitchen and get myself a plate. Whatever she has fixed smells absolutely amazing. Her house smells like a Mexican restaurant. "I'm starving. I haven't had anything to eat since this morning."

She bends over to get some silverware out of the drawer. I want to grab her ass, but we can save that until later. "I don't know how you could wait so long to eat. I think I would have passed out."

I wouldn't go that far, but I was pretty fucking hungry. "Let's just say I've had a very eventful day."

I wasn't about to go into details about my day, because I can't. I would never involve her with club business. They were things she didn't need to know about. Things she would never know about.

She doesn't ask me any questions and I'm thrilled that she doesn't. "I spent my day cleaning because I didn't want you walking into a dirty house. It's the reason I didn't take a shower and do my hair earlier."

I press my lips against hers and give her a kiss. "You couldn't have known that I was going to come a little early."

She opens up her eyes and stares into mine. "No, but I'm glad that you did, because it is such a nice surprise."

Now is the time to address how much I disliked her door being left unlocked. Anything could have happened. "Jaycee, I realize it's summer time and it's not yet dark out, but please don't leave your door unlocked. Anybody could have come in, and I don't want anything to happen to you."

She walks away from me to get the taco scoops out of the cabinet. "You really think someone would really come in here and do something to me? I thought the dangers of that happening would be so much less here than living in the city. I've never felt in danger and you saying that scares me a little."

I myself have walked into unlocked doors because of the club. It makes killing people and fucking them up so much easier. We don't make a lot of noise and we are always quiet. They never see us coming and can't get away.

"The last thing that it should do is scare you, Jaycee. You can never be too cautious."

She opens up the bag of scoops that are sitting on the table, then gets out the shredded cheese from the fridge. "I have a gun I keep in my bedroom and have had ever since I lived in Sweetheart Bay. Nothing ever did happen. I just wanted to keep it for protection."

That makes me proud to hear her say that. Now I won't worry so much about her.

Since we are on the subject of guns, it is time for me to tell her about always having a gun on me. I don't want her to be freaked the fuck out when I got mine out of my pants. "I always keep a gun on me. The only reason I didn't have a gun on me yesterday was because I had just gotten out of jail."

She looks at me, uneasy, clearly wanting to change the subject. "I made us some chicken salsa. I really wasn't sure what you would want. I was going to make us some cupcakes but didn't have the time to."

I can't wait to dig in. "It looks amazing." This wasn't something I had tried before. "I guess you don't cook much since you work at the Grill. I know that I wouldn't, especially if I had to cook there."

I dip out the chicken, salsa, peppers, corn, and onion into a bowl. Then I head over to the table and pour myself some cheese. I top it off with crumbling the taco scoops, even though I know you're supposed to scoop the salsa and chicken.

"I love cooking, especially when I have you coming over."

I don't know if being too sweet is a thing, but if it were, she would be it.

I take a bite of my food, not caring that it burns my mouth. "You are a good cook. This stuff is delicious."

"Thank you. I'm not the greatest cook." She gets two beers out of the fridge before handing me one. I open up the beer and take a drink. It does wonders to cool off my mouth. "But I do try. It is hard to mess up anything when you put it in the crockpot."

I scarf down the rest of my bowl and then get up to get another plate. "It doesn't matter that you put this stuff in the crockpot, because even then I would mess it up. I can't cook worth shit. I could eat ten bowels if this stuff, it's so fucking good."

She laughs. "If you eat ten bowls, then we won't be able to go in the bedroom later."

Did I hear her correctly? Was she already talking about going in the bedroom?

Maybe it isn't such a good idea to get ten plates after all. Two was going to be enough. "We will still manage to go to the bedroom. Don't you worry about that."

She blows on her food before taking a bite. "I thought maybe you had some big plans and were going to stand me up."

I sit down at the table with the bowl in my hands. "I don't know why the hell you would think that." I pour more cheese on the food and crumble up the taco scoops. "You think I would stand you up after the great night I had? You must be crazier than hell."

"I just thought that's what outlaws do." She picks at her food and then looks over at me with curiosity in her eyes. So being an outlaw was what had drawn her to me. I didn't like that much because that was how me and Natalie started out. "I don't know. I figured that you had some business to take care of, business that was more important than having dinner with me."

I don't even know where to begin. "Jaycee, the boys do come before everything else because they are my brothers. That is the way things are always going to be. It's not like I wouldn't have called you if something came up. I just don't have your number."

"Well, that's something that needs to change." I have my own personal cell phone that I take with me to work and when I run errands, but no other time. All the other times I would have disposable phones, because I don't want to get caught committing crimes. "I will give it to you before you leave."

"You better not forget."

"I don't want things to be weird between the two of us when I ask you this question."

"Things aren't going to be awkward between the two of us, Jaycee. I can tell you that right now."

She gazes into my eyes and it burns all the way down to my soul. "Do you see me as something as long-term?"

Why did she have to ask this now? Right now, the only thing on my mind is to have a little fun.

"What do you mean by something long-term?" I need clarification, because to me she could be talking about two different things. "I can tell you right now I'm not the marrying kind."

"I'm not talking about getting married, silly. I'm just talking about something more than what's going on between us now. Am I always just going to be someone that you hook up with?"

I could tell her what she wants to hear, but I decide to be honest. "I can't tell you that right now. It's too early on. I can say that I wouldn't sleep with another woman if I'm hooking up with you."

She seems satisfied with that answer. "That's something we can both agree on, because I don't plan on having sex with other men either. Not that there's anyone else I plan on having sex with but you."

I know where she is coming from when she says that. In this town it doesn't take you long to figure out who everyone is. It doesn't take you long to nose around in their business to find out more about them.

"Good, because then I wouldn't be able to come visit you."

I would become outraged seeing her in bed with another man. It would be like living a life with Natalie all over again. So that definitely wasn't going to happen. I wouldn't allow it to happen.

Her lips form into a frown. "I don't understand how people can hook up with multiple people at the same time. Like, if sleeping with only me isn't good enough, then you can just kiss the two of us hooking up goodbye."

"Have you ever hooked up with someone before this?" I only ask the question because I didn't want to break her heart if we quit doing this. Not that I would want to quit doing this any time soon.

She nods. "I have this one other time, but the guy turned out to be a real jerk. He was screwing around with other girls. I walked in on it and ended things with him. Let's just say that things were pretty awkward."

I may be many things, but I would never do that to her. "He sounds like a real asshole."

"He was, but I don't think about him anymore." I am glad. She doesn't need to think about him anymore because I'm the one occupying her bed. "You know, I turn thirty on Halloween and have only had sex with three people my entire life. I feel like that's kind of lame, considering my lack of sexual experience. One guy even turned me away because I wasn't experienced enough for him."

To me, that isn't lame at all. It made me want her so much more. "The guy must have been a real dumb ass not to realize that he was missing something great. Last night you gave me the best blow job I've ever had."

"I have been practicing with a banana so that I could get it just right."

I finish eating and I'm done with talking. I want nothing more than to be inside of her. I have to get back to the clubhouse before it gets too late.

"What do you say about showing me around?" I suggest.

She takes off her dress, revealing her bare breasts. It's almost like she's read my mind. "I don't want to make it to the bedroom. I want you to take me right here."

I grab everything that is sitting on the table and set it on the counter. "I've been thinking about fucking you all day long."

I might still give her a chance, but I'm not getting emotionally attached right now. I just want a woman that I can fuck senseless. A woman that would hopefully be able to take Natalie off my mind.

She comes over to me and wraps her arms around my neck. "To be honest, I have too, and that's the biggest reason that I'm glad you showed up. Let's just say that pleasuring myself has gotten old real quick."

I can't help but laugh at her saying that, because it's so true. "Glad that I am able to help you with that."

She presses her lips hungrily against mine and I squeeze her breasts. Moans escapes from her lips. "You touching me feels so good."

I take off my shirt and leather cut, then place the gun on the counter. "Tell me what you want me to do to you."

She sits on top the table and spreads out her legs. "I want you to make me scream."

I pull down her panties and move two fingers around inside of her. She is already soaking wet for me. The only thing I want her to do is relax, so that she can enjoy every single moment of what I am about to do to her.

I stare at her breasts and then run my tongue down to her stomach. I continue making my way down her body and kiss the inside of her thighs to tease her. Her eyes close and I hope she's concentrating, letting the rest of the world fade away.

I grip her thighs, then press my tongue inside of her.

Her back arches, and she moves her hips in a circular motion, begging me for more. I continue moving my fingers inside of her and suck on her clit. Screams of pure pleasure come out of her mouth.

I take off the rest of my clothes and move inside of her. After several seconds of sliding in and out of her, the two of us begin to move together. Pleasure runs through my veins and I gaze into her eyes. Natalie's face pops up in my mind and she has a smirk on her face. It's then that I know I have to kill her in order to move on.

Jaycee's entire face falls when I stop moving inside of her. "Did I do something wrong?"

This is what I have been looking forward to the entire day and now I can't finish. I start putting on my clothes and grab my gun from the counter. "You didn't do anything wrong, Jaycee. I just have a lot on my mind and think that it's best if I go."

She gets up from the table and straightens up her clothes. "Don't go. The two of us can talk and I can put us on a movie. I don't need to have sex with you, Pete. I enjoy your company."

"I can stay for an hour, but not much longer than that."

Her entire face lights up. "Come sit down in the living room and I will find us a movie to watch."

I make my way into the living room and the only thing that I can think about is killing Natalie. I want her to feel the pain that she has made me feel. I don't give a damn what the club has to say about it. My mind is already made up and nothing is going to stop me. She needs to die.

# TWENTY-FOUR

# CASH

REAPERS WINGS BAR AND GRILL'S parking lot is empty when I walk through the door. I feel like absolute shit for not getting Darcy lunch earlier, so I am going to make her a salad. I walk to the back. Andrew looks like he's tired and worn out, probably from the rush earlier.

I get a salad bowl from behind the counter. "By the look on your face, I would say that it's been busy."

Andrew nods. "It has been nonstop ever since four. Thank God things have slowed down now, or I don't know what I would do."

There are tables that still have dirty plates on them. Mud is caked in some places on the floor. When I reach the salad bar it is nearly empty, but enough for me to make Darcy a salad. "You should have called in another person."

Andrew shrugs. "I just let the phone hang off the hook for a couple of hours until we got caught up."

That's one way of doing things, though I didn't do it often.

I fill up Darcy's salad with lettuce and vegetables. "At least we are getting the business."

"There will never be any complaints there."

The phone rings, putting an end to our conversation.

I notice a car pull up in the parking lot, then Natalie hurries inside. I wonder why she is here, but I'm about to find out. She looks around the restaurant until she finds me. There is urgency in her voice when she speaks. "Thank God you're here."

"What's going on?"

She licks her lips and fidgets with her shirt. "I'm damned any way that you look at things. I didn't know Liam was part of the Southern Demons when the two of us got together. Being together with him is a mistake I will regret for the rest of my life."

The funny thing about it is I don't feel any anger towards her anymore. I feel sorry for her because this club can't help her without going behind Pete's back. I can't say that I completely trust her, either, because I don't have a reason to.

"What do you want from me?" There isn't a reason to drag out this conversation. I need to get back to Darcy.

"Hugh doesn't know I am here." She takes out a piece of paper from her pocket. "This is where Liam lived during the couple of months he was here. I figured this would maybe help you in finding him."

I take the paper from her hand and put it in my pocket. "Why are you doing this?"

"Because he's a disgusting excuse for a human being. I didn't know how evil he was until I seen what he did to Darcy. Then later what he did to me, and I'm sorry I didn't stop what happened."

"Darcy said you saved her life, so you have nothing to be sorry about."

She nods. "I was wondering if you think that Pete could ever forgive me."

This was probably the real reason she had come here. "Pete's together with Jaycee now, so I don't think he ever could."

Her face falls the minute I say Jaycee's name. "I don't know where I'm going but I've got to go."

I watch her leave and wonder what her real intentions are. I'm sure it won't be long until I find out.

———

Martin greets me when I walk in the door. "I'm glad you're here. Darcy has been in the bedroom for a couple of hours. I think she is asleep, but I'm not sure. I didn't want to disturb her."

I pat him on the shoulder. "Thank you for staying with her."

"It's no problem at all. Would do it again in a heartbeat if you need me to."

"I'll let you know everything that is going on a little later." I head towards my bedroom. "Darcy needs me because I won't be staying here with her tonight. A lot of shit is about to go down."

"Don't worry about Darcy. You can count on me to keep her safe."

I am so very thankful for him and all of my brothers. I couldn't ask for a better family, even if we aren't blood. "I know you will. That's why I consider you more like a brother than a cousin."

Darcy looks up at me when I walk in the door. She lets out a yawn and I hate that I disrupted her sleep. "Babe, you didn't have to go get me supper."

I hand her the bag of food that is in my hand. "That's where you are wrong, because I did. I didn't give you lunch like I promised earlier today, and I hope that this makes up for it."

She opens up the bag and gets the salad out. "I was starting to get worried about you, since I haven't heard from you all day."

"I've been busy looking for Laken, but we didn't find her." It hurts my soul to say those words, but she has a right to know. "That's one of the reasons why I'm not going to be able to stay the night with you."

She doesn't hide the disappointment on her face. "I'm glad you came here now, because I was starving. I hate you aren't going to be here tonight, but I know you've got to do what you've got to do."

One of the things I love about her is how she's so understanding. "I'm not going to stop searching for any of them until they are dead. It's the only way I will be able to sleep at night, knowing they are no longer walking this earth anymore."

She pours the ranch dressing on her salad and then puts the lid on it to shake it up. "Not just any girl can say they have a boyfriend who is willing to kill for them. It makes me so proud to call you mine."

"Sweetheart, no one is ever going to hurt you and get away with it."

She eats her salad and doesn't say anything for several minutes. "I talked to my mom earlier today and told her about what happened. It's time to make amends with her. I can't do this with her anymore. There's no use in the two of us fighting. It's time we made up. I couldn't imagine her not being a part of our children's life."

It makes sense she needs her mother now more than

ever before. "I am proud of you for talking to her, because you needed to."

My mind gets to thinking about Nancy and our argument earlier. I wonder if she's really going to move, or if that's just something she threatened to do. Either way, I can't make amends with her. I don't want to make amends with her if she can't accept me for who I am.

"I guess it will be out of the question for a while, but maybe one weekend we can go down to Sweetheart Bay. I would really love to visit with her before they move back. The beach will do me some good."

I kiss her forehead. "Maybe we'll be able to when this entire thing blows over."

She finishes eating her salad, then rests her head against my chest. "I really hope that maybe turns out to be a yes."

"I really hope it will turn out to be a yes, too, sweetheart."

"I hate that you have to go back out tonight." She glances up at me and presses her lips against mine. "I was wanting you all to myself."

I run my hands through her hair. "I promise you will get me all to yourself once Liam, Laken, and Hank are dead."

She closes her eyes and makes herself comfortable. "I can imagine our babies now. I can't wait to be pregnant. I'm going to stay at home with them if you let me, and everything is going to be perfect."

I can picture our babies too. I hope we have girls so they can't be a member of this club. I couldn't bear to think about losing a son because of club life. Then I would never able to live with myself. The worst part about it would be my relationship with Darcy would be ruined.

"Of course I will let you stay home with them,

sweetheart. I wouldn't want anyone raising our babies but you."

"I want you to do something for me." She opens up her eyes and stares so intently into mine that I wonder what this is about. "Don't be mad at me when I say that I want you to make up with Nancy. She's your mother and has a reason to worry about you."

This isn't a conversation I want to have. "I promise you I will take that into consideration."

"That's the only thing I am asking."

She runs her hands underneath my shirt and I take off my leather cut. I set it down on the chair, then sit back down in bed again. I stare into her pain-filled eyes and want nothing more than to make love to her. I know without having to ask that it's something she wants.

I take off her shirt and then run my hands along the front of her breasts. I unhook her bra and she throws it down on the floor. A hint of a smile forms on her face. "I want us to try to make a baby, Cash. Since you can't be here with me later, it's the perfect time right now."

I run my fingers across her nipples and she lets out a low moan. I hover over top of her and kiss her hungrily. The need to consume every single part of her makes my erection throb against me.

I pull my shirt off over my head and she runs her hands across my bare chest. The anger that I have bundled up inside pours of my soul. Right now, the only thing that matters is making Darcy feel alive inside. It's about making her feel pretty fucking good despite her pain.

She unbuttons my jeans and I push them down to my ankles. I pull off the rest of her clothes and then make myself comfortable between her legs.

I suck on her thigh and she giggles. Her entire face lights up. "I love when you do that," she says.

I grin back at her. "I know you do, sweetheart, that's why I always love doing it."

She runs her fingers through my hair and I press my lips against her pussy. "How did you know that I needed a kiss?"

I don't answer her because I press my tongue on her outer lips and stroke. Moans escape from her lips, and I massage her pussy with my tongue. She clings to the bedsheets and screams erupt from her lips.

I kiss her hungrily and then run my beard across her face. She laughs before gathering my face in her hands. The minute I walked in, pain was on her face. That pain has been replaced with hope. Hope that soon we can make a baby and finally start our family.

I pull down my boxers and stroke inside of her. She puts her hands around my neck and I gaze into the soul of the woman I love so much. The woman that I refuse to live without. This life that I'm living would be nothing without her.

I move inside of her fast and she works her hips along to keep up with me.

"Go a little slower, babe," she mutters.

I stroke deep inside of her and put my hands on her hips to guide her along. Sweat trickles down both of our faces as we move towards one another. We finally reach that sweet spot and I cum inside of her.

Her breathing is heavy and a grin is on her face. "Have we got time to cuddle before you get back?"

I lay down beside of her. "I wouldn't dare leave without getting cuddles from you, sweetheart."

I watch Darcy sleep for the longest time before getting out of bed. I put on my clothes and before I leave the room, I plant a kiss on her forehead.

Martin is in the living room, watching TV. "I'm glad that you stopped by. Darcy has been dying to see you."

"I felt like a shitty boyfriend for coming here and not bringing her anything to eat earlier."

Martin dismisses my comment. "The last thing you are is a shitty boyfriend. Hell, Pam and Nancy were both here, so they cooked. You were out there getting justice for Darcy and making her proud."

"I didn't find Laken or the rest of them."

I hate saying it, because it makes me feel like a failure.

"I'm sure you will find them. I wouldn't worry about that too much."

I hope so. I am ready to focus on starting a family with Darcy.

"Speaking of Pam and Nancy. Here they come now."

Pam and Nancy both make their way over here. There doesn't appear to be any tension between the two of them and that's a good thing. I have never known the two of them to get along.

Nancy walks in the door first and sees me. "I'm sorry for slapping you across the face earlier. That was uncalled for. I love you and I promise not to talk about things that upset you anymore."

It takes everything inside of me to muster the words I say next. "Don't worry about it, Nancy. I love you too."

Pam looks from Martin to me. "You can go out with Cash tonight. I don't mind staying here with Darcy."

Martin shakes his head. "That's not going to happen. What if something happened to you?"

Pam folds her arms across her chest. "You're going and I

don't want to hear another thing about it. I know how to take care of myself and have been doing it for years."

Martin and I both know this isn't an argument we're going to win. Darcy is going to be in good hands with Pam. The last thing Pam is afraid of is pulling the trigger.

# TWENTY-FIVE

# PETE

I STOP down at the marina before heading back to the clubhouse. My motorcycle is hidden out of sight from public view, so no one knows I'm down here. I can't go to the clubhouse right now. I have to be alone. I need to put a plan in motion for how I'm going to kill Natalie. I want to put my hands around her neck and choke the life out of her. It sure was fun seeing the fear in her eyes earlier today. I will have to call her sometime and lead her out somewhere to get her alone. Then I can go through with it. Killing her will be a piece of cake.

I see a car pull into the marina, then Laken gets out. Her hand is bandaged up and she has a book bag on her back. Holy fucking hell. Cash is going to be a happy man tonight. The person he has been looking for is right in front of my eyes.

I dial his number and he picks up on the first ring. "Get your ass down here at the marina. Laken is here."

"Keep an eye on her and don't let her leave. I'll be there in a couple of minutes." I can hear the happiness in his voice.

———

CASH

I park my motorcycle next to Pete's, then walk down to the marina where Laken is sitting at a picnic table. The minute she hears my tennis shoes hit the pavement, she looks up at me. The fear is all over her face. She knows I am going to kill her tonight, and I won't ever regret it either.

"You're a hard woman to find," I say.

She gets up from the picnic table and starts walking down to the lake. "You must not have looked hard enough, because I've been around."

Pete comes out of the shadows to make it known she doesn't have anywhere to go. "I don't know why the fuck you would come down to the marina. It's pretty fucking stupid, if you ask me, knowing very well that Cash has been looking for you."

She takes a deep breath and stutters when she speaks. "I came down here because I'm getting ready to leave. I was just waiting for someone to come pick me up and take me to the airport."

I'm just glad she didn't make arrangements earlier. Then I would have never been able to see her right now. "Where do you plan on going?"

Tears stream down her face. "Rehab to get help with my drug addiction."

I have heard this so many times before and there's no way I believe it now. "You're not going anywhere anymore, Laken, because you will be dead in your grave. I don't know if you believe in Heaven or Hell, but you're going to meet your Maker."

Sobs escape from her lips. "I'm sorry for what I did to Darcy."

I laugh. She isn't sorry. The only thing she is sorry about is me going to kill her now. "You're just telling me you're sorry because you don't want to die. I've got news for you. The minute I saw you with Darcy last night, my mind was made up. You played a part in trying to kill the most precious thing to ever happen to me. Did you think that I could possibly just let you walk away?"

Pete goes along with what I am saying. "I know I sure as hell wouldn't. I would kill her the exact same way she tried to murder Darcy."

I glare into Laken's eyes. "I'm nicer than that Pete, because I am just going to kill her execution style. I am just going to make it quick and easy."

Laken takes off running down to the lake and I shoot her in the shoulder. The bullet goes clean through and she falls down to the ground. "I have a son who will never know who I am."

I lower the gun to her temple. "That's just too damn bad. Maybe he will be adopted to a good family. A family that doesn't consist of a bunch of junkies."

Her lips tremble and she stares up at me. "He needs to know me because I'm his mother. I promise to turn my life around. Please just let me go and I will never set foot here in Heartwood Springs again."

That's not good enough. It will never be good enough.

My Darcy will forever be traumatized.

"What good would it be to have a junkie as a mother, Pete?" I ask.

Pete shakes his head. "None, if you ask me. The kid will have less problems if she's dead."

She grips onto my jeans and her entire body is shaking. "Please, I'm only thirty and have my entire life ahead."

Pete peels her off of me and kicks her in the ribs. "Keep

your hands to yourself, you fucking bitch. It's not going to help save your life."

I have heard enough.

I laugh, then glare at her. "Have you got any last words?"

Helpless sobs escape from her chest. "God, please forgive me for all my sins."

Goodbye, bitch.

I shoot her point blank in the head and she falls to the ground. A puddle of blood forms around her body and near my feet.

Now if only we could celebrate tonight.

Relief washes over me, because she's finally dead.

Pete pats me on the back. "One down, two more to go."

It feels good hearing him say that. Liam and Hank can't be far, and I can't wait to find them, then pull the trigger.